LAST SECOND CHANCE

A Christian Suspense Novel

ROBERT GOLUBA

Published by Evertouch Publishing, an imprint of Evertouch Inc.

Gilbert, Arizona

ISBN 978-1-7330513-1-6 (Print)

This book is a work of fiction. Names, places, characters, and incidents are the product of the author's imagination. Any resemblance to actual events or places or persons, living or dead, is entirely coincidental.

Bible quotations are from the New International Version (NIV).

Copyright © 1973, 1978, 1984 by International Bible Society

Edited by Laurel Garver

Cover Design by Stephen Novak

For new release updates, exclusive content, promotions and freebies, sign up for the email newsletter at: RobertGoluba.com/newsletter

For the people that ask, 'What if?' and 'Why not?'
Two simple questions; four words; twelve letters that open doors to infinite ideas, opportunities, and solutions.

ACKNOWLEDGMENTS

Thank you to Lauren Goluba. The toughest, yet most helpful beta reader I know. You helped make *Last Second Chance* better. A special thanks to Laurel Garver for your editing skills and patience with my writing flaws. You helped make FireSky Ranch a reality.

CHAPTER ONE

Rick Powell clenched his jaw until it was sore. His dream could be ripped away, one birthed twenty years earlier when he started his agency.

Rick rushed past the elaborate paintings and well-appointed décor of Austin's premier office tower. He dodged a small group of men and women shaking hands and greeting each other in the lobby. Once at the bank of elevators, he pressed the up arrow. Beads of sweat formed on his forehead as he paced in front of the closed doors.

How could Todd just vanish on today of all days? They'd worked together on their presentation for weeks and Todd knew the importance of this meeting. There was no way for Rick to match his poise and people skills presenting new advertising campaigns. In the early years of the agency, Rick tried to take the lead on presentations, and failed. He was too direct and impatient. Too proud of his work. What did it matter if the ideas were mostly his if he bored the audience with every minute detail or worse, offended everyone in the room by defending his work when a potential client voiced any criticism?

The elevator door opened, and Rick was inside within two seconds. He punched the thirty-eighth floor and hit the door close button in rapid-fire succession. As the open doors released their grip, a hand reached in and prevented the doors from closing. It was Julia, his creative manager.

"Good luck," she said.

"He should be here. I can't believe he'd pull this kind of stunt today."

"Don't let it get to you. You've got this, Rick!"

Rick flashed a half smile and vanished behind the elevator doors. He'd experienced many losses in his life and worked hard to avoid the penetrating sting of another.

Rick's stomach lurched as the elevator ascended, carrying him up to a global technology firm. If they won the account, Omega Enterprises could put The Longhorn Group into the top ten of all advertising agencies in Austin. The dream was close enough to touch, but Rick sensed it slipping away. He needed Todd, but he was missing in action. Together they made The Longhorn Group a formidable team. Today, Rick had to present solo for the first time in decades.

After someone exited the elevator on the twenty-second floor, Rick felt warmth climb up his back to his shoulders. Though he was alone now, the elevator felt smaller than a doll house. He rotated his head several times like a boxer before a fight. His mouth was dry, and his throat constricted when the elevator doors opened to the ornate Omega Enterprises sign. His feet felt so heavy that he stopped in front of the Omega door and noticed the blurry reflection of his ashen face in the glass. He straightened his tie, took a deep breath, and entered the office.

Two hours later, Rick reappeared in the lobby where Julia and her assistant Addy had been waiting. They rushed past the leather couches and glass coffee tables to Rick. His tie was loosened, shirt untucked, and hair ruffled on the right side from his hand raking through it the whole ride down.

Rick looked toward Julia and Addy, but left as fast as he had entered. He strolled through the revolving door without saying a word. What was there to say? "Kiss this year's bonus goodbye"?

Rick slithered his six-foot frame into his white BMW. He pushed the ignition, lowered the windows, and rotated the dial to Drive. He pressed the gas pedal closer to the floor and the engine purred. His short wavy hair flopped in the wind tunnel inside his car.

They promised him a decision within a week, but Rick didn't need an official response. He already knew the answer. The dream nearly close enough to grasp was a mirage. Todd's absence cost Longhorn any chance of winning the Omega Enterprises account.

A headache marched from the back of Rick's neck into his temples. He rubbed them with the index and middle fingers of both hands while driving with his knees. Rick couldn't afford a migraine now. Once he found a suitable playlist on his iPhone. he tried to push all thoughts of Todd and Omega from his brain.

After lead-footing a typical half-hour commute down to twenty-five minutes, Rick passed the house where his wife was waiting for his arrival. He continued to the south end of FireSky Ranch, parked and meandered down the gentle sloping banks of Half Moon Creek. Rick deposited himself on a picnic table that had supported four generations of the Powell family. Closing his eyes, he listened to the soothing sound of the water as it trickled down the channel carved through the rocks over decades. The throbbing in his head subsided. When his eyes opened, the shadow from the creek bank had darkened the narrow body of water.

He rose from the picnic table and trudged back to his vehicle. Before he climbed in, Rick Powell put the world on notice: "Never again. No more partners. I will start a new agency and it'll be the best in all Central Texas!"

A flock of startled blackbirds released their grip on the branches above and flew away.

Minutes later, Rick pulled into the parking lot of a dove white, two-story farmhouse with a wraparound porch. His wife Felicity was in the kitchen cutting a slab of beef into smaller portions for the smoker.

"So?" Felicity asked as she put the knife down and washed her hands. "How'd it go?"

"Not good. Todd didn't even show up."

"What? Did he know how important Omega is for the company?"

"I don't know. We haven't been seeing eye to eye lately. Revenue is flat and Todd wants to lower our rates to go after smaller accounts and get more volume. I want to maintain our focus on quality and target adding one or two large accounts. Omega was our chance to land a giant and we lost it."

Felicity crossed her arms and shook her head. "I don't get it. Why would he be a no-show for such an important presentation?"

"I hope to find out soon, but now I'd like to stop talking about Todd. I may set a new record for my blood pressure."

Felicity leaned over and wrapped her strong, slender arms around Rick's waist. Her head fit comfortably below his chin. Leaning on his chest, she said. "I'm sorry, honey. I know how important this was to you."

Rick kissed Felicity on the side of her head. Strands of her straight, wispy hair clung to his goatee. "It's going to get ugly next time I see Todd."

The next morning, Rick woke an hour before his alarm went off. He wasn't hungry, so he took a stroll through the stables as the crew fed the horses eager for their breakfast. Rick exited the south stable and was nearly hit by a bale of hay hurtling from the loft to the hay rack below.

"Hey, watch where you're throwing!"

He looked up to identify the culprit, but instead of a burly stable hand, he saw a tanned, wiry, gray-haired woman.

"Mom! You should let the guys do that."

"The guys work harder for me when they see me jump in and

get my hands dirty once in a while." Elizabeth had been general manager of FireSky Ranch for the past two decades, taking over the role from her father-in-law—Rick's grandfather—after he passed suddenly from a heart attack. Rick sometimes worried that his mother might suffer a similar fate from the physical and emotional pressures of running the place.

"I don't want you to get hurt doing something like that."

She threw another bale down to the stack growing on the trailer.

"How'd it go with your presentation yesterday?"

"Not good."

She paused, head tilted in concern. "Why, son? What happened?"

"I still need to get ready for work, so I don't have time to talk about it now. I came out to see if you want to go to the lake house with us next weekend."

Rick's mother jumped down and took off her work gloves.

"Are the kids going?"

"Yeah, I'm forcing them to go since they're both graduating this year."

"I'd love to, but I promised Sergio he could have off that weekend. Maybe next time."

He hated to think of his mom stuck home alone for the weekend in the first-floor in-law suite of the house she shared with Rick and Felicity.

"Sorry, Mom. I promise we'll find a second weekend when you're able to join us all."

Everyone but Todd was hard at work in the cozy office at The Longhorn Group, the ad agency Rick and Todd founded twenty-two years earlier. Many times in the past, the small staff had heard the raised voices behind Rick's or Todd's closed doors, but were as dumbfounded as Rick about Todd's disappearing act. They'd recently begun whispering amongst themselves: was

Todd sick? Had he quit? Was he fired? Could a partner get fired?

The tension was thick. It hung in the room like the humidity after a July thunderstorm in Austin. Heads swung to the front door anytime someone walked in. As two days turned to four and then five, their anxiety level waned.

A full week after Rick's Omega presentation, the silhouette of Todd darkened the front door. The hum of the fluorescent lights was deafening as Todd made for Rick's office.

"We need to talk."

Rick motioned to his door. "Shut the door and sit down."

"No thanks. I'll stand."

Todd closed the frosted glass door behind him. He stood in front of Rick's desk.

Rick reclined in his leather, high-back chair behind the desk and crossed his arms.

"Do you care to explain where you've been the past ten days? Your disappearance cost us the Omega account."

Todd put his hands in his pockets and looked at the floor. "I needed some time to think."

"During a presentation to the largest client we've pitched in a half dozen years? You know we present best as a team."

"That's what I was thinking about."

"Thinking about what?"

Todd took a step toward Rick and put both hands on his desk. He leaned in, "Rick, this isn't working out. We want completely different things for the future of this business. I want to invest in providing more services to smaller businesses, so we're not held hostage by a few large accounts. You want more of the large accounts that I want to get away from."

Rick tipped his chair toward Todd. "We can't maintain our superior quality standards if we cut our rates to attract the small businesses that you want. I think that would be a huge mistake."

Todd shrugged. "I'm fine with it."

"That's crazy, Todd. Why would we sacrifice our reputation of high-quality design that took us decades to build in order to attract accounts that can't afford to pay us?"

Todd stepped back from the desk, standing taller. "I can't do this anymore."

"You can't discuss business strategy?"

"I can't keep fighting you on the direction to take this company. We both want to run Longhorn our own way and they're not compatible."

Rick rose from his seat and walked around his desk. He stopped near Todd and leaned up against his light birch wood desk. "What are you suggesting?

"Either buy me out or we dissolve Longhorn and go our separate ways. We can each start our own firms and run them the way we want to."

Rick narrowed his eyes and set his lips in a thin line. "What do you have in mind for a buyout?"

Todd located a pen and a pad of paper on Rick's desk. He jotted down a number and slid it across the desk.

Rick looked at the offer, crumbled up the paper and tossed on his desk. "Are you nuts? That would deplete every penny from my savings. No way!"

"Then we only have one option. We'll dissolve The Longhorn Group."

Rick stood motionless as Todd laid out all the steps. "I'll file the forms with the Texas Secretary of State and confirm we have no outstanding tax liability. If you absolve me from any financial or legal liabilities, I'll let you keep all the staff and clients."

"Now I know what you were really doing the last week and a half. You must really want out."

"I do."

The response caught Rick like a sucker punch in the gut. His chest tightened and words were hard to produce. After a dozen uncomfortable seconds, Todd broke the silence.

"I'll withdrawal half of whatever is left in the Longhorn account in sixty days and close down the account. Then you'll be free to do whatever you want. It's been a good ride, buddy. I truly wish you the best of luck with whatever you do next."

Todd turned and left without saying another word. He was past the front door before most of the staff could even look up.

Rick leaned back in his chair and examined the expanding crack in the ceiling. Two minutes later, he exhaled and left his office. The entire staff—now huddled around Julia's desk—all looked up when they noticed Rick. He guessed they all had the same pit in their stomach as he did.

Rick felt the heat of their gaze on him. "It's been a long week, so let's get the weekend started early. We'll start fresh next week. See you all on Monday."

In truth, he wanted an empty office when he called his accountant and attorney to discuss his next steps. Rick scheduled meetings with both for Monday morning. He wondered if he should cancel the trip to the lake house in order to focus on the situation and mull all his options.

After short consideration, Rick shook his head. Time with Felicity and the kids at the lake would recharge him. "I need it more than ever right now," he said aloud.

The sense of loss hit Rick on the drive home, but it didn't sting as he expected. With each passing mile, a sense of relief and hope for future possibilities grew.

CHAPTER TWO

Rick's weekend took a turn for the better as soon as he
turned the corner into FireSky Ranch. His son Cody was
placing fishing poles into the trunk of Felicity's SUV while his
daughter McKenna was pushing a large blue cooler into the back
seat. It was almost time for another Powell family weekend at the
lake house. They may not have many more opportunities with
Cody set to graduate from college and McKenna from high school
at the end of the school year.

Two hours later, Lyndon B. Johnson Lake and its grayish blue
water dominated their windshield. A few twists and turns later,
the familiar cream hue of the brick lake house appeared. The four-
bedroom single-level home with eighty feet of direct lake access
has hosted Powells every year since Rick's father purchased it
thirty years earlier. Rick guided the Ford Explorer down the short
asphalt drive. As soon as he cut the engine, both kids shot out of
their seats and sprinted down to the water's edge.

The view of the lake from the driveway reminded Rick of his
father surprising them with this wonderful vacation home. This
vista was Rick's first view of the place that day. He'd sat in the
back bench seat of the Ford SuperCab truck with his brother and
sister. He nearly lost his breath when his father pulled into the

9

driveway and the massive lake came into full view. He never forgot that feeling.

Jack Powell Sr. was only able to visit his new retreat once before he died, but Rick cherished the memories from that weekend. Rick spent sunrise to sunset with his big brother, Jack Jr., in the canoe fishing and exploring nearby lagoons in LBJ Lake. Rick's relationship with Little Jack was better at the lake house. In the three decades since then, he wondered if they'd ever again be as close.

Rick turned his attention from the lake and helped Felicity unpack the snacks and beverages. He transferred the cold cans to the refrigerator and met Felicity on the back deck. They adjusted the Adirondack chairs on the deck for an unobstructed view of the lake. The angle of the September sun splashed light across the surface of the lake and through their iced tea glasses.

They sat watching Cody and McKenna try to push each other into the water from their standing paddle boards. Despite Cody's seven-inch advantage on McKenna, she held her own. She was scrappy like her momma.

Felicity was the first to break the silence. "I can go back to work full-time until you get traction with the new agency. Dr. Shelton's office was very happy with me as their office manager before the kids. Maybe he could find something for me."

"Thanks, honey, but you're invaluable to Mom on the ranch. Plus, I feel good about the new plan I'm putting together. With Todd out of the picture, I should be able to keep all of our clients and key members of the team like Julia. I can focus on picking up a couple of new accounts that appreciate the level of support and quality we'll deliver."

Felicity reached over and put her hand on Rick's. "Okay. Just remember that I can and will help if you need it."

Rick squeezed her hand and turned his attention back to the kids. Cody tumbled into the cool waters of LBJ Lake and McKenna raised her oar high in victory.

Rick wanted to spend more time relaxing, but when the family went out for ice cream, he was stuck inside hammering out his plan for his next venture. He had to be prepared for the meeting with his attorney and accountant Monday morning. He also needed to have a plan to share with the Longhorn staff.

Sunday, they returned to FireSky Ranch, arriving after the shadows from the grand live oak trees engulfed the entire front yard. Elizabeth was on the porch, curled up in her favorite chair reading a book. Rick slid a chair across the wood planks and sat next to her.

He shared the news about his meeting with Todd and his plans to start a new agency of his own.

"I'll make it one of the top agencies in Central Texas."

Elizabeth flashed a half smile and looked back down to her book.

"What's wrong?"

"Nothing."

"Mom, I can tell something is wrong. What is it?"

Elizabeth put the book down. "I'm happy for you. I truly am. Just sad that I'll be the last Powell to run FireSky Ranch."

Rick's grandfather, Wayne Powell, was a respected Texas rancher. Quarter Horses was his specialty. He built FireSky Ranch fifty-two years earlier to host horses, trainers, and riders at this outpost in the hill country southwest of Austin, Texas. The sprawling ranch covered one hundred and sixty-eight acres of prime grazing pasture with live oak and cedar elm trees dotting the rolling hills. Elizabeth raised her three children on the ranch and had lived there over forty years. But none of the children got the ranching gene. While the oldest, Jack, was an animal lover, he decided to become a veterinarian and moved to Kansas City to join his father-in-law's practice. The middle child, Cassie, loved the land—selling it, that is. She had become one of the top real estate agents of land, farms, and ranches in Hays County. And Rick, the youngest, was the arty dreamer who turned his creative mind to advertising. He was the least likely of the Powell kids to stay on the farm, but there he was.

Rick left his chair and knelt next to her.

"Felicity and I aren't going anywhere, Mom, and we can find a great general manager when you're ready to retire. Maybe even make some of the improvements I've been suggesting for years."

Another half-smile. A tired one.

"I hope you create the most awesome agency south of Dallas."

"Thanks, Mom."

Monday morning arrived like an unwelcome guest. Rick hit snooze twice. He laid in bed another five minutes after he turned off the alarm. He skipped breakfast and replaced it with an extra cup of coffee at the office. The anxious looks from the staff as they entered the office did not go unnoticed by Rick.

After his accountant left, Rick met with his attorney for nearly two hours. As the attorney rose and exited, Rick looked at the clock on his computer. It was 11:23. He couldn't delay the news any longer.

Rick sighed and left his office to announce, "Let's all meet in the inspiration room. I have an update to share."

Once they all found their favorite spots on the couches or one of the colorful bean bags, Rick shared the news. All employees will be paid for the next two months as they continue to support their clients and The Longhorn Group will close after Thanksgiving.

"This had nothing to do with you. It was due to a disagreement among the founders that could not be resolved. Therefore, I'd be happy to provide a reference or help you secure your next job."

Discussion broke out among everyone in the inspiration room. Rick waited for the conversations to die down. They needed time to process what he'd already accepted.

"Does anyone have a question for me?"

Addy raised her hand and then stood up from her lime green beanbag.

"What do you plan to do after Longhorn shuts down?"

Rick stroked his goatee for a couple seconds.

"This is a new development for me too, so I'm still finalizing my plans. I've owned an ad agency most of my adult life and design is what I do well. I'm sure it will be something related to an agency."

The team exchanged glances and turned back to Rick.

"Well, if nobody else has questions, we still have clients we need to keep happy."

The small group dispersed. Rick caught Julia as she passed his office.

"Hey, Julia, got a minute?"

"Sure," she said as she closed the door behind her.

Rick stood behind his sit-stand desk. Julia sat down and swept her jet-black locks behind her ears.

"Julia, I'm starting a new agency. I'm going to run it the way I've always believed Longhorn should have been all these years. We won't chase every new social media or technology trend like Todd wanted to do. The new agency will focus on great design in all mediums and we'll target firms that understand and appreciate the benefits of superior design. Focus is the key, not chasing every shiny new object."

Julia shifted her weight. "Makes sense."

"You sound unsure."

"The plan sounds great and I agree with the focus on design, but what about presenting to clients? That was always Todd's job. Won't he try to take our best accounts to wherever he lands?"

"Legally, I don't think he can, at least as far as I understand the terms of how we agreed to dissolve the partnership. I'll be working with our attorney to get the new agency setup as fast as possible and then reach out to each account. I think…"

Rick paused and glanced out the window in his office.

"I don't just think, I believe most of them will see the value in our quality and support."

"What about presenting and pitching new accounts?"

Rick paced behind his desk.

"That's the reason I want to talk to you. I'd like you to be part of the team as the first creative director. Not only do you have respect for deadlines and an eye for design, you're also articulate and clients are drawn to you. You can do everything Todd did, but better. The two of us will present together as a team."

Redness filled Julia's cheeks as her smile widened. "Thank you for the kind words and for considering me."

"You've earned it."

Rick circled his desk and extended his hand to Julia, "Will you be my creative director?"

Julia stood and shook his hand. "How soon can we get started?"

Rick laughed. "I love that spirit. Let's get started right away."

"What are we going to call the new agency? Have you thought of a name yet?"

Rick moseyed back to his chair and dropped in. The chair rolled back until it hit the wall. Rick looked up and then smiled, "JWP Group after my dad and grandpa."

"I love it."

Over the next four weeks, Rick and Julia met with clients and shared the new vision for JWP Group. The response was positive, and the new agency was prepping for take-off right after the new year.

The looming birth of JWP Group was going so well that Rick and Julia planned to open a new office. It would reside in a space befitting a premier advertising agency in Austin. Their real estate agent secured a preview of an office in a complex built the prior year in southwest Austin. The third-floor suite felt more like the top of a plateau with its wide-open floor plan and sweeping views of the Hill Country outside the floor-to-ceiling windows. A sprinkling of gold and rust colors dotted the distant landscape as a preview of the show Mother Nature had in store after a recent cold snap.

"Julia, I could totally picture my office in this corner. It would be hard to concentrate on work with these views, but I could power through it."

Julia laughed. "I know, right? I'd put my desk up against this window."

Rick removed a tape measure and some masking tape from his backpack. He measured one direction and then another. He pressed one end of the masking tape down and walked away from the window. He repeated the process with another long, perpendicular piece of masking tape.

Julia tilted her head, "What are you doing?"

"I'm laying out my office." Rick pointed. "One wall will be here and my door will be over there."

"Can I borrow that tape?" Julia put strips of tape on the industrial olive-brown carpet. It filled half of the empty suite.

Rick watched Julia with amusement. "I'm lost. What's all that?"

Julia stood up and eyed her maze of masking tape. "I'm going to put production over there. I want them to be close to the graphic design team and the copywriters. Quality assurance will be right next to me. This layout will provide the most efficient workflow for all our projects."

Rick clapped. "I love it. I'm glad you're on my team."

Rick's phone buzzed in his pocket. He saw it was Felicity and answered.

"You need to get home as soon as possible," Felicity said. "It's your mom."

"What's wrong?"

"I found her unconscious on her bathroom floor. I don't know if she fainted or what happened, but I can't wake her. I called for an ambulance, and it will be here any minute."

CHAPTER THREE

The twenty-minute drive to the ranch felt like an eternity. The sight of an ambulance in front of the FireSky farmhouse made Rick's stomach knot up and sent adrenaline rushing through the rest of his body. He thought of his dad and his grandpa. An ambulance has never brought good news.

Rick shuffled toward the house, his chest tight. As soon as his foot hit the end of the sidewalk, the front door opened.

A paramedic backed out with a gurney and moved to the porch. She was followed by another paramedic squeezing an oxygen bag. They pulled belts over the patient for a secure trip down the steps and to the ambulance. Rick couldn't see his mom, but the outline of a person under the white blankets was exactly the size of Elizabeth Powell.

Rick waited at the bottom of the stairs. When the gurney was on the sidewalk, the paramedics stopped, and Rick moved closer. The paramedic removed the oxygen bag and Rick saw his mom. Her face was nearly as white as her hair and her eyes were closed.

Rick's knees felt wobbly, so be backed away. His mind raced with questions. Did she have a heart attack like grandpa? Will she live? Will she ever open her eyes again? What will happen to her?

The paramedics resumed oxygen for Elizabeth and pushed her

down the sidewalk to the back of the ambulance. Felicity caught up with Rick.

"How is she?"

"They think she may have had a stroke. She's breathing and has a pulse, but she's still not responsive."

Rick stood behind the ambulance, dizzy with shock. What would he do without her? He ran his fingers through his hair as the medical team neared the open ambulance doors. Rick placed his right hand on Elizabeth and whispered a quick prayer. *Please, God, please save my mom. We still need her here*. He clung near the gurney until the paramedics raised Elizabeth into the ambulance, then hooked her up to several medical devices.

The driver met Rick and Felicity at the back of the ambulance.

"Are you related to the patient?" she asked.

Rick stepped forward. "I'm her son."

"Are you going to follow us or ride with us?"

"I'm going to ride with you." Rick climbed in. He found Elizabeth's hand under a blanket and held it tight.

"Where are you taking her?"

"Saint David's South Austin Medical Center," the driver replied.

Rick scooted to the back of the ambulance and called to his wife, "Felicity, please let Cody know, and when McKenna gets home from her FFA meeting, come up to Saint David's. I'll see you there."

The crunch of the tires over the gravel echoed throughout the ambulance as it creeped up the road leaving FireSky Ranch. Rick moved to the end of the bench seat to provide ample room to the medics. He wanted them to do their best work on this patient. They checked the numbers on their monitoring equipment and asked Elizabeth multiple times if she could hear them.

She didn't respond.

Rick stared at his mother's pale, motionless face. He pursed his lips, curled both hands into fists and pounded on his knees while shaking his head.

She couldn't leave us now. She was just working on the ranch. She couldn't leave them with no warning like Grandpa did. She just couldn't.

He looked up at Elizabeth. "Come on mom, be strong."

Tears welled up.

Rick wiped his eyes when he heard a beeping noise, and a red Emergency sign grew larger in the back window. Several people in scrubs were waiting behind the ambulance. As soon as the back doors opened, those people swept his mother out of the ambulance and wheeled her past the double doors.

Rick looked at his watch. Twenty-five minutes and still waiting to be called into ER admissions.

"Rick Powell" came from a tired voice behind the counter.

"It's about time," Rick muttered. If Mom was conscious, she was probably wondering where her family was.

Rick signed everything without reading. He slammed his pen down and stood up. "Which way to the ER?"

"You're not done yet, Mr. Powell. That was just for the insurance. I have more waivers for the hospital."

"Are you kidding?"

The admission specialist had dark circles under her eyes. She pulled her graying hair back from her face, but did not respond. She stared at Rick until he found his seat and pen.

After he signed eight more forms, Rick rejoined his mother's side. He sat silent while doctors and nurses examined Elizabeth. Four episodes of *Friends* later, Elizabeth's primary doctor, Dr. Pavlock, informed Rick that they plan to admit his mother into Intensive Care.

"I'd recommend going to the ICU waiting room on the third floor. You'll be more comfortable there." Dr. Pavlock tapped a few buttons on her tablet.

"Do you know what's wrong with her?"

"It looks like a stroke, but we're are running tests now. I'll let you know more as soon as I do."

The ICU was on the third floor so Rick took the elevator and found the ICU Waiting Room. Felicity was there with McKenna. Rick's sister Cassie with there with her entire family of six. Everyone stood up when Rick walked in.

"How is she?" Cassie asked.

"She's stable but still unconscious. They believe it was a stroke, but still have tests to run. It'll be a while before we know for sure."

"Little Jack will be here in a few hours. He's catching the next flight down from Kansas City," Cassie shared with the group.

"So glad he's able pull himself away from work to come down here."

"Not now, Rick," Cassie huffed.

"Mom's lying unconscious in the ICU because she's been running a ranch for the last twenty years. Wasn't that supposed to be Jack's job? He was groomed to take over by Dad and Grandpa and then left when a better opportunity in Kansas City popped up."

Cassie leapt up. She leaned over Rick in his seat and pointed mere inches from his face.

"I said 'not now.' Not here! It's also his mother is lying in that bed. He's not coming down here to get in a fight over a decision he made two decades ago. He's coming to support his mother. Just like you!"

Rick glared at Cassie but said nothing. He'd seen streaks of red in her eyes before. He slumped in his chair and turned away.

Felicity heard the argument and moved next to Rick.

"Honey, I'm sorry about your mom. But it's not Jack's fault."

Rick kicked his feet forward and leaned back in his chair. He gave his attention to the ceiling for a few seconds and exhaled loudly.

"You're right. I hate that my mom is fighting for her life and I guess I'm looking for someone to blame. I'm okay now." He glanced toward his sister. "Sorry, Cass."

Cassie rose and returned to her previous position in front of Rick. When she looked him in the eye, her lips quivered and tears brimmed. Gravity won and tears streamed down her face.

Rick stood up and hugged Cassie. They both cried.

Cody arrived at ten. Jack joined the other Powells just after midnight. Cassie, Felicity, and McKenna gave Jack Jr. a hug when he walked in, while Cody shook his hand. Rick remained in his seat until Jack walked over to him. Rick stood up and extended his hand.

Jack leaned in and embraced him. "You're getting a hug whether you like it or not, you stubborn mule. I haven't seen you in over a year."

Rick's remaining anger faded away.

Cassie caught Jack up on their mom's condition and everyone shared highlights of their past year. Yawns started to spread around the room.

"It's getting late," Rick said. "Jack, you can go back out to the ranch with Felicity and McKenna to get some sleep if you want."

"You deserve some rest, Rick, I just got here, so I'm fine staying."

Even with his mother clinging to life in her hospital bed eighty feet down the hall, Rick couldn't help competing with Jack, a decades-long tradition.

Nobody left the waiting room.

The next morning, not long after everyone began to stretch and stir in the waiting room, Dr. Pavlock appeared.

"Powell family?"

Twenty-two sets of eyes turned toward the doctor.

"Good news. She's awake."

A collective exhale filled the room, and everyone exchanged hugs. Dr. Pavlock explained that Elizabeth had a stroke and that they would conduct additional test to understand the full extent of her damage. No visitors were allowed to spend time with Elizabeth until she had a full day to build up her strength.

Rick, Felicity, and their kids sat along one wall and Jack Jr. and Cassie's family sat along a perpendicular wall. Everyone but Rick and Jack hopped back and forth to talk and play card games. It was like they staked out their own territory in their respective corners of the waiting room and didn't dare to leave it unattended.

Jack told Cassie he was going to find a doctor to get an update on Elizabeth.

"I talked to Dr. Pavlock earlier. What do you want to know?" Rick offered.

Jack cleared his throat. "I'd just like to ask a few more questions with the doctor."

"She told me everything they know. What else do you expect to learn?"

Jack looked over at Cassie and she lowered her head.

"Rick, we know that you're very creative, but you aren't always the best with details. I'd like to talk to the doctor to be sure we're aware of everything they know about Mom."

Rick leaned back and crossed his arms. "Knock yourself out." He shook his head as Jack left the waiting room.

The next day, everyone was watching the entry into the ICU waiting room. They jumped up in unison when a doctor entered, but it was for another family. Hours after everyone finished breakfast, a man in a white coat entered the waiting room and asked for Elizabeth Powell's family. A new doctor was on duty.

The doctor shared the test results that confirmed that Elizabeth had suffered a severe stroke paralyzing her left side. Her future would include intensive therapy to regain basic skills like dressing herself, bathing, and eating. The doctor said it was unlikely she would walk again.

The doctor handed Cassie a brochure with *How to Transition a Parent to Assisted Living* printed in bold black letters on the front. He said an assisted living facility would be the ideal place for

Elizabeth to receive all her needed therapy and live a happy and productive life.

"The good news is that Elizabeth is feeling stronger today and if she is up to it after lunch, you can all pay her a visit."

Everyone sat back down. Cassie pulled her two nearest children next to her and hugged them. Jack positioned his elbows on his knees and planted his face into his hands. McKenna leaned her head on Felicity's shoulder. Rick caught the glisten of her tears rolling down her cheeks. McKenna would sorely miss her trail rides and fireside chats with Grandma.

Rick focused his attention on the carpet between his shoes. He wondered how the same woman that was slinging bales of hay easier than men half her age was leaving FireSky Ranch.

Nobody said a word. One by one, they all left the waiting room. Rick was one of the last to leave. He decided to snag a snack in the hospital cafeteria. As he perused the yogurt cups and drinkable smoothies, he found Cassie and Jack standing by the fresh fruit in an animated conversation. Rick tiptoed over to investigate the bananas, out of their line of sight but able to hear everything.

"I can't move down from Kansas City, but I may be able to run the ranch with some help."

"What about Sergio? Can he do it?"

"He's capable, but he's content as operations manager and wants no more responsibility than that. In fact, he'd like us to look for his replacement soon. He told mom last year he wants to retire."

"I guess I can also help out, but real estate can be very streaky. Sometimes it will be hard to commit."

"It will not be easy, but Mom needs to focus on getting better. We need to take this off her plate."

Rick dislodged a banana from the heap without detection and scurried back to the waiting room. He sat in a corner and tapped his finger on the armrest.

· · ·

Later that afternoon, they lined up to visit Elizabeth. Per the doctor's recommendation, they took turns to avoid overwhelming the family matriarch. Elizabeth's children choose to visit youngest to oldest.

Rick entered the room first. Elizabeth's eyes were open. He stood to the side as Cody, McKenna and Felicity went up to Elizabeth and gave her a gentle side hug. They were careful not to disturb the copious number of tubes and wires hooked up to her.

McKenna moved first to Elizabeth's side.

"Grandma, I got my goat to do a great show walk last week. I may have a good chance at the state fair next month. I can't wait to show you how well he does."

Elizabeth turned her head and blinked several times.

Felicity moved behind McKenna. She moved McKenna's wavy hair to the right and peeked over her daughter's left shoulder. "I started reading the book by that new author you'd been telling me about, Elizabeth. It's really good. Thank you for the recommendation."

Felicity slipped an arm around McKenna's waist, watching Elizabeth expectantly and listening to the rhythmic beat of the equipment hooked to her. The open, warm eyes of Elizabeth was the only response they needed.

After his wife and kids had their visit with Elizabeth, Rick kissed his mom on the cheek. The right side of Elizabeth's lips curled slightly, but she said nothing. Rick squeezed her hand, and she squeezed back. Rick continued to hold her hand until Cassie and her family entered the room.

All the families had dinner together in the hospital cafeteria that evening. After dinner, small groups split off in different conversations. Jack and Cassie moved across the aisle to another table. They had the brochure for assisted living lying on the table between them. Rick joined in the conversation.

"I found the perfect place for mom," Cassie shared. "It's called Gentle Breeze. It has everything she'll love, especially their game room. They told me it's a hot spot to play cards and other games. Plus, it's not too far from Rick or me."

"Sounds like a great fit," Rick chimed in.

"Great find, Cass," Jack said. "Thank you for all your help on this. I have to head home tomorrow, so we need to keep working on the general manager for FireSky."

"I have a client coming in from Arizona who wants to look at several ranches tomorrow, so I'll be leaving tomorrow morning. Did you ever get in touch with your old classmate from vet school you thought would be a good fit?"

"Yeah, he moved to Tennessee, so that's not an option," Jack said as he scrolled through his phone. "I'm sure I'll find somebody who could be a general manager. I'm just drawing a blank right now."

Rick opened his phone. He scrolled through several beautiful pictures on Instagram. He tapped the heart to like a picture of a sunset with wispy, colored clouds over LBJ Lake.

"I'll also ask some of my former clients to see if they know anyone they would recommend," Cassie contributed as she also scrolled through her phone.

Jack set his phone down and shot up from his chair, "I know someone who would be perfect for the job."

"Who?" Cassie asked.

Jack returned to his seat. He leaned back with his feet on the table and his hands folded on this stomach. "Rick Powell."

Cassie and Jack turn to Rick as he looked up from his Instagram feed.

Rick could feel the color from his face disappear like a rabbit in a magic show. "I'm starting a new agency," he protested. "Now is not a good time for me."

"My family and practice are in Kansas City and Cassie has way too much on per plate already with family and real estate. Can't you put the agency on hold or do both for a while?

"You're the horse expert, Jack. Why don't you run FireSky? You got all the training with Dad and Grandpa growing up. You were taught how to do everything. Oh yeah, I forgot. You moved to Kansas City when the going got tough. "

Jack snapped back, "You're already living there, Rick. You wouldn't have to uproot your family or juggle a business in another state. You're ideal for this. You just have to be willing to learn."

Rick paced between the tables. He glared at the expectant looks from Cassie and Jack, then slammed down in his chair and crossed his arms. It was like Jack and Cassie still viewed him as the fifteen-year-old boy who struggled to cope with the loss of his father— not mature enough to see the big picture, needing their guidance.

"I can't believe this. I've got the least amount of experience running a ranch and I'm trying to start a new business to save one that's closing. I don't have enough time. I can't do this." Rick kept his arms crossed and muttered under his breath.

After a minute of silence, Jack and Cassie made eye contact. Cassie turned to Rick, tilted her head and smiled. "You *can* do it Rick. Will you?"

Rick looked over to Jack and back at Cassie. Seconds later, he huffed a heavy sigh, "Fine, I'll do it for Mom, but it's not a lifetime commitment. I'll keep FireSky on track until we can find someone else."

Cassie stood up and hugged Rick.

Jack sat with his arms crossed.

CHAPTER FOUR

Rick woke up in his bed on the second story of the farmhouse like he'd done thousands of times before. However, this day was unique. He'd be looking at the ranch through the eyes of a general manager. The guy in charge. The feeling was foreign to Rick, although it was something he thought about often over the years.

He visited every corner of the property, inching along as he took mental inventory of every building, animal, machine, and plot of land. His creative mind was at work with ideas for improvement.

After spending a full day surveying the ranch, Rick invited Felicity to the kitchen.

"I have some important news to share with you."

Felicity sat down at the kitchen table. Rick pulled out a chair and sat down across from her.

"Cassie, Jack, and I talked at the hospital. We came to an agreement that I'm going to be the new General Manager for FireSky Ranch for a while until we can find somebody else."

Felicity's brows lowered. "You won't be able to start your new agency. Are you sure that's what you want to do?"

Rick leaned back in his chair and put both hands behind his

head.

"It's more of a need than a want. I told Jack and Cassie that I wouldn't be a permanent solution, but it would get us through this transition. It's important that someone in the family lead FireSky now. Plus, I can execute some changes, like new stables and pens that I've been recommending for years. I'll turn FireSky into a profit business for years to come. I can start JWP Group once I'm able to hand off a healthy FireSky to a new general manager."

Felicity put her elbows on the table and twisted her hair. "How long are you thinking?"

"I think I can get everything ready to hand over within a couple of years. Three years max. Once the new stables are built and leased, they'll generate enough income to hire a decent general manager. With my marketing and advertising expertise, I feel confident I can do it in two years.

"Then you'd start your new agency?"

Rick sat up straight and puffed out his chest. "Yep. Until then, it's time for the next generation to take over FireSky Ranch."

"What happens if something goes wrong, and it doesn't work? What's your Plan B?"

Rick tilted his head and widened his eyes. "I don't have a Plan B. I work my tail off to succeed at whatever I put my mind to. I'm doing this for my family. I'll succeed or I'll die trying!"

"Okay." Felicity reached across the table and squeezed Rick's hand. "If you're committed to make this work, I'm in too."

As Felicity rose to leave the kitchen, she stopped and asked, "Have you told Julia?"

"I will soon. I don't know how she'll take it."

Two days later, Rick joined Julia and her former assistant Addy at their favorite coffee shop near the Longhorn Group's old office. Julia was dressed in business casual attire, her sandy fawn sweater in stark contrast to her pinky brown lipstick and ebony hair. Rick wasn't sure if Addy owned any business attire. Though she graduated from the University of Texas three years earlier, she still dressed like a student, perpetually wearing Vans shoes, ripped jeans and t-shirts from summer music festivals.

It was a cool day and the coffee shop was crowded. After they stood near the entrance for a minute, Julia saw several students close their laptops and she pounced on the table while they packed. They claimed their table by slinging coats on the back of chairs and setting bags on their seats. They made small talk as they stood in line.

After they each ordered a hot concoction from the barista wearing skinny jeans and a rainbow-colored beanie, Rick shared the news that he was putting JWP Group on hold.

"Why? What happened?" Julia asked.

"It's only temporary, but I've been pulled into the family business. I'm going to be running FireSky Ranch full time now that my mom is in assisted care. I need to build up the business and stabilize it so we can hire a general manager before I can start JWP."

Addy chimed in, "My family used to own a small dairy farm until we sold it and now my dad is working with his brothers and sisters flipping houses."

"So how was it? Working with family?"

"Mr. Powell, do you get along with all your brothers and sisters?"

"My sister's great. My brother, not so much."

"You'll probably want to change that if you want a successful family business."

While Rick sat gaping at Addy, Julia piped up, "How long do you think it will take to get the ranch on track?"

Rick raised his eyebrows, shook his head to regain his focus and turned to Julia.

"A couple of years. Not too long."

"So, what's your plan?"

Rick scooched his chair closer and leaned in. For the next ten minutes, Julia and Addy listened to the business plan to make FireSky Ranch the gold standard in Central Texas.

When Rick stopped long enough to take a breath, Julia announced, "I've got to get to another appointment, so I'd better head out now."

They put their coats on and packed up. Rick hugged both women and held the door open as they left the coffee shop. Addy waved and turned left to the parking lot.

Julia turned to Rick after she was past the closing door. "I want to be part of JWP and would love to show what I can do as a creative director, but I have bills to pay. I'm going to have to find something else. Just know that I may not be available forever."

Rick nodded. He had to pray she found a good-for-now job. So much of his dream for the agency depended on her.

As the new general manager of FireSky Ranch, Rick didn't just want a healthy business, he wanted a thriving business. He told his mom and grandpa numerous times they should invest more in resources that would generate additional revenue, like pens and stables. Elizabeth joked how easy it was for Rick to say "it takes money to make money," from the safety of his ad agency office.

Now, he was in charge. One of his first decisions was to build a new stable and double the number of stalls from sixteen to thirty-two. Rick calculated that leasing out the stalls in the new stable would generate the required income to hire a full-time general manager and get his dream of launching JWP Group back on track.

After receiving multiple bids from contractors Rick had found online and deeming their prices too high, he received a referral from a neighboring rancher. Rick met the contractor and showed him the land south of the current stables he envisioned for the new stables. The contractor examined the grounds and took measurements. After he finished, the contractor met Rick in the parking lot.

Standing between their vehicles, Rick said, "Give me an estimate once you've completed all your measurements and renderings. I don't want to go back and forth on price, so shoot me your best price and I'll let you know if you get the green light."

"Sure thing," the contractor chuckled.

Rick looked around and pointed to his chest.

"Did I say something funny?"

The contractor tried to suppress his smile but was unsuccessful.

"No, you didn't say anything funny. I know you come from a long line of ranchers, but I rarely work with guys in penny loafers and pastel shirts leaning up against his wife's BMW."

"This isn't my wife's car."

The contractor chuckled again and spit tobacco onto the cracked dirt.

"I'll get you a fair final estimate in a few days."

The contractor fired up his truck and leaned out his window. "If you want to be taken seriously as a rancher, you might want to rethink your look. A little less country club, a little more country, if you catch my drift."

Rick stood frozen in the parking lot as the contractor left, his diesel truck belching exhaust from its chrome smokestacks between the cab and bed. He retreated to the house and stood in front of the full-length mirror that Felicity used to verify her fashion sense.

The man in the mirror had a pressed, pastel green dress shirt with a buttoned collar. Dark navy-blue jeans were held up with an auburn Italian leather belt. Rick did not observe a rancher in the mirror, but an owner of a hipster ad agency.

The next day, Rick crossed the threshold of one of Austin's finest men's western wear shops for the first time. He purchased a pair of cowboy boots fit for a fifth-generation Texan. Days later, he traded in his BMW sedan for a new set of wheels. A Ford F-250 Platinum XL with a crew cab and an extended bed. Rick sat up tall with grin so wide that oncoming traffic could surely see his smile while driving home in his new tank. He honked when he pulled into the parking lot in front of the farmhouse.

McKenna was first on the scene. She gawked and asked, "Is this *yours*?"

Rick walked around to the other side of the truck next to McKenna. "Yep, I picked him up today."

"This is super nice, Dad. What did you name him?"

"I haven't thought about a name yet. What do you think I should name him?"

McKenna skirted around the ruby red truck, caressing every curve as she rounded each corner. "Big Red. No doubt, he's a Big Red."

"I love it. Big Red it is!"

Sergio Garza, assistant manager and the best teacher of all things FireSky, led Rick through months of daily on-the-job training as a rancher. He had worked on FireSky Ranch for 22 years with all three Powell generations.

Rick required a thorough education on modern ranching. He knew the basics like feeding and grooming from growing up on the ranch, but Sergio had to teach him everything else he needed to know. Sergio educated Rick on all the tack and gear, as well as ranch hand responsibilities. He showed him how to use all the equipment and tools to repair and maintain the ranch. He even gave Rick a roping lesson that was supposed to take a day, but it turned into a week-long exercise. Rick had to hope no horse ever got loose, because roping was not his strong suit.

After Rick graduated from Sergio University, he tackled the construction of the new stables, training pens and operational changes at FireSky Ranch. He executed his marketing and advertising plan to fill the new stables. Rick continued to learn as he was immersed in his role as a rancher. His education continued as he learned from a plethora of mistakes.

CHAPTER FIVE

Eighteen months after becoming the general manager of FireSky Ranch, Rick Powell's life was dramatically different. The weight of the ranch on his shoulders made it hard to catch a full breath. Everything was riding on him and he needed guidance. Rick fired up Big Red.

Five minutes later Rick arrived and slid out of his truck. Once he passed the ornate gate, he walked one-hundred thirty-four steps. He was aware he could shave off ten steps if he cut the corner near the Stevensons' plot but didn't dare.

At step one-thirty-four, he kneeled and caressed the etching on the smooth granite monument. A birth year, a death year, and a name: Jack C. Powell Sr.

Rick twisted, sat and leaned his back against the gravestone. The familiar position and the coolness penetrating his back helped Rick relax. He wiggled his fingers into a baseball glove. After thirty-two years, it was easier to get them inside the narrow holes designed for a fifteen-year-old. He made a fist and punched inside the glove a few times. His father had taught him to punch his glove before every play to show he was ready for the ball. Every play, Rick dutifully punched his glove and glanced to his dad in the stands, except the day Jack Sr. missed his game because of the accident.

Rick threw pebbles with his free hand.

"Dad, why does it have to be so hard?"

The only response was from a crow perched high atop a cedar tree like a sentinel in a Medieval guard tower.

"Dug myself a deep hole this time."

Another pebble landed past Rick's feet.

"It'd be nice if you and grandpa were still around to help."

Rick dropped the last of the pebbles.

"Don't worry, I'll figure it out."

He pulled his feet in and hugged his legs as he watched the shadows grow longer and darker on the well-manicured lawn. Rick inhaled the aroma of the fresh cut grass and closed his eyes. After a silent prayer, he rose to his feet.

"I guess it's time I get back to work and face the music."

Rick stood up and turned to the headstone. "Talk to you later, Dad."

He patted the top of the monument with his baseball glove like he always did since his father was buried there three decades ago. A tombstone fist bump of sorts. It was a ritual Rick held dear after his father's traffic accident.

Rick paused at the adjacent plot. Its marker displayed a death date twelve years after Jack Powell Sr.

"Bye, Grandpa."

Back at the farmhouse, Rick climbed the stairs to his home office. He peered out the window and flipped through a stack of mail he'd been avoiding. He stopped when he got to a thick envelope with a bright red stamp.

Rick lowered and tightened his eyebrows; then he released an emphatic sigh. He flung the letter the length of the office onto his weathered oak work desk with the grace of a Vegas blackjack dealer.

"Past Due? Get in line!"

Rick turned his attention to the world outside his window. He surveyed the new stables and training pens. Then his gaze turned to the rolling hills sloping into the tree line near Half Moon Creek at the south end of FireSky Ranch. He could feel the gravity of love and labor invested by two generations of Powells before of him like a weight vest on a scuba diver.

Rick extended his arm and placed his hand on the wall next to the window to support his weight. He lowered his head and slumped his body. After half a minute, he looked up and a cloud of dust in the round pen caught his eye. A horse was dragging the lunge line behind him while circling inside a pen. The vet was out two weeks ago after a mare tripped on a line and injured her leg—an injury that Rick vowed would never happen again.

"You've got to be kidding me!"

Rick raced to the round pen. He slid in the gravel and slammed into the fence to stop. Then he yelled to his ranch hand Blake, "What the heck are you doing?"

"Don't worry about it," Blake said without turning around.

"I told you not to drag the lunge line, and this is the third time I've seen you do it."

Blake kept his eyes on the horse rounding the pen.

"Blake, you saw what happened two weeks ago. I don't want another vet bill!"

Blake snickered. "Lighten up, man. It's not a big deal."

In a single bound, Rick hurdled the fence and emerged behind Blake. He grabbed Blake's arm just above the elbow. "Get your stuff and get out of here. You're done."

Blake spun and lurched toward Rick.

"What did you say?"

Rick grabbed Blake by the collar with both hands and pushed him up against the fence. The clang of a body impacting a metal fence echoed throughout the stables. Blake countered by securing Rick's shirt in both fists.

Looking down at Blake's red face and flaring nostrils, Rick

growled, "You heard me, Blake. Get outta here. You no longer work here!"

Blake shot back with a scowl and then he released Rick's shirt. He threw his arms up in surrender. "You got it, boss!"

He spat and strutted over to his backpack.

"You're an idiot, Rick, and you have no clue how to run a ranch. Never have, never will. You need help bad. Really bad. You're gonna regret this."

"Go on, get out of here!"

Blake tossed his bag in the bed of his truck as he climbed in. He spat again and revved the engine, his tires spewing gravel as he sped off.

Rick stood silent as the truck of his former ranch hand disappeared behind a billowing cloud of dust on the parched Texas road.

Felicity emerged from inside the stable.

"What's going on?"

"It's impossible to find good people to work here."

"Who's the problem now?" Felicity asked with her chin out and hands on her hips.

"Blake! I told him not to drag the lunge line, and he kept doing it. A horse tripped on one a couple weeks ago and I had to call the vet. Blake knows better."

"Well, that didn't take long. He's only been here a month. We can't keep burning through people like this."

"I can't keep paying people who aren't getting the job done! We can't afford to do that anymore."

"How bad is it, Rick?"

"Not now, Felicity," he snapped. "I've got too much to do."

Felicity stomped into the house, and Rick stormed into the stables.

Rick's next victims were a few innocent hay bales. After a few body blows and a roundhouse punch, Rick collapsed into the hay and cried out "Can't I ever get a break?" Several horses stirred in their stalls.

Blake's biting words hung in Rick's mind like a dense fog. For a second, he wondered if Blake might be right, but it didn't matter. Rick had to make this work. Too much was at stake.

After stewing for several minutes, he threw his work gloves and left the stable.

Rick drove down to the south end, the southern edge of FireSky Ranch, to monitor the grazing horses.

An hour later, during his expedition back to the stables, Rick's phone rang on the seat next to him. He saw it was Ryan, his business account manager from Lone Star Bank. He waited until the fourth ring.

"Hey, Ryan, what's up?"

Ryan was a fast talker and started this call at warp speed, "Mr. Powell, thank you for taking my call. I've been trying to reach you for a few weeks now. Did you get the overdraft notices in the mail?"

"I'm a few weeks behind on mail."

"I'm sorry, Mr. Powell, but my boss is getting on me to get this resolved. Our overdraft protection for your account has covered three checks over the last two weeks, but your account still has a negative balance. Do you have anything available in another account you can transfer?"

"Everything is pretty tight right now."

"I understand, Mr. Powell, but we need to resolve the negative balance as soon as possible."

Rick raised his voice and replied, "We've been doing business with Lone Star Bank for over thirty years. Can I get something to you in a few weeks?"

"Hmm," Ryan paused. "Mr. Powell, have you considered liquidating assets? Do you own any underutilized equipment or land you could sell?"

Rick was silent for several seconds as he rolled down the washboard road. A Rolodex of broken-down equipment flashed through his mind, but how would he get top dollar for any of it?

"I've heard of some neighbors selling land for a nice premium lately. I have a small plot that may work so I'll look into that."

"Great idea, Mr. Powell. I'll send you names of a couple of appraisers I'd recommend so you can determine the value of the land."

"Okay."

"Have a good day Mr. Pow—"

Rick hung up the phone and threw it on the empty passenger seat. "When it rains it pours."

CHAPTER SIX

The next morning, Rick woke up after the first rays of sun penetrated the bedroom. He brewed a cup of oil-black coffee and joined his canine companion Rocky in the kitchen. He made scrambled eggs, toast and added fresh ham from a local family farm. Rick plated the feast and took it to the kitchen table. He patted Rocky's head and went outside to the garden to get the final touch to complete his breakfast surprise.

Rick stood in the bedroom doorway with his tray of piping hot deliciousness. "Honey, are you awake?"

Felicity sat up in bed and craned her neck to get a better view of the fresh country breakfast. "Is that a rose? That's so sweet! You didn't have to do this."

"Yes, I did," Rick said as he placed the tray on the nightstand. "I snapped at you yesterday, and I'm sorry."

"Thank you." Felicity scooted to the middle of the bed and patted the vacant area next to her. "Come over and sit with me."

Rick sat down next to Felicity. She pulled her strawberry blond hair into a ponytail. It highlighted the emerald green of her eyes and the dim freckles on her smooth face. Rick fell for those same features twenty-six years earlier while they were both students at the University of Texas.

She took a sip of coffee. "You seem stressed out. Is everything okay?"

Should he tell Felicity how bad it was? He didn't want to stress her out over his mistakes that he was sure he'd fix soon. No, he'd better keep the shaky financial situation to himself for now.

"I'm still trying to figure out this ranch. I thought for sure that building the new stables would have helped. It's not in my blood like it was for my dad and grandpa. I always knew I was the black sheep of the family," Rick said with a grin.

Rick worked on FireSky Ranch next to his older brother and sister when he turned eleven, but he never developed the passion for ranching like the others. He preferred to swing off the tire into Half Moon Creek at the south end and draw in his sketchbook. His passion for drawing and graphic design led him to his Visual Communication Design degree at the University of Texas and the birth of The Longhorn Group.

"You were never the black sheep, Rick. You have different strengths. You're creative, and you spent the last twenty years at an ad agency, not a ranch."

Felicity slid one hand under Rick's hand and put her other hand on top, "Maybe you should focus on getting FireSky to a place where you can hire a general manager as soon as possible."

"That's the plan. I need to get FireSky running on all cylinders so I can get back to building my agency."

"Be sure to find a partner better suited for you next time."

"Or no partner. I would have been better off running The Longhorn Group by myself all those years. It's hard to find people you can trust these days."

Felicity dropped Rick's hand and lowered her eyes. Rick caught her look.

"I'd need to find someone good enough to satisfy Cassie and Jack."

"Would your family ever feel comfortable with someone who's not a Powell?"

Rick ran his fingers through his hair, "Yeah. Um…it's possible. I'd just need to find the right person."

Felicity finished the eggs and rolled out of bed. "I need to get up and look after those two geldings with eye infections."

"Okay, I've got a hot date with a broken faucet in the wash stall."

"Would you like a hot date for lunch?"

Rick gave her a quick kiss. "I'll be there!"

After Rick replaced the broken faucet, he was testing it for leaks when he noticed a truck coming down the gravel road to FireSky Ranch. It was Cassie.

Rick put down the tools and wiped his hands clean on the front of his jeans.

He met Cassie in the parking lot and hugged her when she got out.

Rick leaned up against her truck, "What's up, Cass?"

"Not much. I'm showing a property ten minutes from here, so I thought I would come a little early and see how everything is going with you. How's Felicity and the kids?"

"Everyone's great. Cody just started a new job in Dallas, and McKenna aced all her finals last month."

"How about Mom? Have you seen her lately?"

"Yeah, I took her to lunch last week, and we played cards for two hours in the game room. It was rough for her moving from the ranch to Gentle Breeze, but I think she's good now."

"Good. Good." Cassie looked past Rick at the ranch behind him.

"The new stable looks great. Is it full yet?"

"No, not one-hundred percent full."

Cassie and Rick both turned their attention to the new stable as if they were waiting for the ivory barnwood walls to clarify Rick's answer.

"Rick, I have a question for you. Someone told me that you

had the back eight at Half Moon Creek appraised. Whatcha doing?"

"Wow, that was just last week. News sure travels fast around here."

Rick fidgeted with the pliers on his worn leather work belt.

"It's nothing. I heard some developers were paying top dollar for land out this way. I was just curious what it was worth, but I'm not selling."

"You sure? That land is special to our family."

"I said I'm not selling it!"

Cassie cleared her throat, "What about Blake Highsmith? I heard you fired him recently."

Rick kicked at a dirt clod with his boot.

"Someone must have you on speed dial," Rick said shaking his head. "He wasn't getting the job done so I couldn't keep him."

"Blake comes from a long line of ranchers who know what they are doing. Blake knows what he's doing. It would be nice to have someone like him working here alongside you and Felicity. You could use the help."

"I know, I know. Trust me, I'd love to have more good help around here. Sergio can't work at FireSky forever. I'm looking, so I'll find someone soon."

"Good to hear. I'm still worried about you, though."

Rick crossed his arms. What was Cassie fishing for?

"Why?"

"You've been in a completely different line of work for over twenty years, and you got thrown into this fast. I want you to know that Little Jack and I are here for you if you ever need any help."

"That won't be necessary, but I appreciate it."

"So how is business, Rick?

Rick kicked a rock between his boots. Cassie seemed to know every detail about FireSky moments after it happened. Did Cassie talk to someone at Lone Star Bank?

"It's slow, but I'm still plugging away," Rick said as he wiped sweat from his brow with the shirt sleeve on his forearm. "I'm not gonna lie. It has not been as easy as I thought it would be, but the new stable and training pen is the answer to hiring a new general manager."

Rick wiped at a dirty spot on Cassie's truck. "Did you really have to show a property near here?"

Cassie smiled, "You know me so well. I wanted to see how you were doing. I do have to show a client property, but it's twenty-five minutes from here, so I've gotta go."

Rick opened the door of Cassie's truck for her, hoping to shake the sting from her lack of confidence in him. He knew he was falling short of his expectations, but he must be falling short of hers too. Has Jack been in her ear?

As Cassie rolled out of the FireSky parking lot, she put her truck in park and leaned out the window, "Hey, Rick? Thank you for doing this. We appreciate it. I know Mom appreciates it. You know Jack and I are always here to help if you need us."

"I know *you* are, Cass."

"Oh, Rick, don't go there. Jack would help, too, if you needed him."

"If you say so. See ya later."

Rick stood in the parking lot until Cassie's truck and the dust trail behind it vanished behind the browning alfalfa on the bluffs.

What else did she know?

Rick checked his watch and found it was nearly noon. He dashed back to the farmhouse.

Felicity was putting the last basket of food on the bistro table on the patio. Rick sat down and Felicity took a hot roll from her handmade woven basket and put it on Rick's plate next to the beef brisket.

"There's more inside if you want it." Felicity sat down. "I'm glad we could have lunch today. It's been a while since you've taken a break for lunch."

"I know. There's always so much to do, but how could I resist lunch with such a beautiful young lady?"

"Good answer, mister."

Rick let out a nervous laugh. The financial situation of the ranch was becoming more apparent to a suspicious eye. It was only a matter of time before Felicity found out.

CHAPTER SEVEN

After lunch, Felicity approached Rick as he washed up in the kitchen sink.

"Rick, if you have time, I'd love it if you could come with me to the grocery store. We're going to the potluck after church tomorrow, and I have a long list of stuff I need to bring. I could use your help."

"Are you going into Dripping Springs?" Rick inquired.

"I need a lot, so I'm going to the big HEB in Austin."

Rick threw down his towel and whined, "That takes so much longer. I still have a lot of stuff I need to finish today."

"I know, but it would be easier for me if you could come and help with the large bags of potatoes and several cases of water. It'll be fast. I promise."

Rick drove Felicity into Austin to get groceries. He made a beeline for the potatoes. While examining each bag like a drill sergeant inspecting his troops, a voice came from the other side of the potato display.

"Mr. Powell, what brings you into town?"

Rick knew the voice before he saw his face. He'd heard it often over the past few months, and that nasally voice was burned into his brain. It was Ryan from Lone Star Bank.

Before Rick could answer, Ryan continued, "I've been trying to reach you. I left you several voicemails since our last conversation, and you haven't called me back. Are you going to put that piece of your ranch up for sale to raise some cash?"

"Ryan, I'm sorry. I should've called you back. I was slammed."

"No worries. Is the land for sale yet?"

Rick straightened up and crossed his arms. "I'm not putting it up for sale. It appraised lower than expected, so selling now makes little sense."

"Wow, that's surprising. I've heard land in that area was selling for a premium. Maybe that appraiser is not as familiar with ranches in Hays County. He should be, though. Anyway, I can get you a referral for another appr..." Ryan trailed off as he scrolled through his phone looking for a number.

Rick placed twenty pounds of potatoes into the cart and said "I don't need it. I'm not selling the property."

Ryan's face snapped up. "We discussed how that might be your only option. At least your best option. What else can you do? If your property goes into foreclosure, I can't help you anymore."

"I'll figure something out, but I'm not selling."

"That's your call, Mr. Powell, but it's still your best option. I think you should reconsider."

"I said I'm not selling!"

Several shoppers stopped and peered over the chest-high mounds of apples, sweet corn, and potatoes at Rick and Ryan.

Rick whispered, "I don't mean to yell. I've got other options I'm working on that will get my account caught up soon."

"I hope so. You're running out of time." Ryan grabbed his cart and disappeared behind the wall of neatly displayed fresh vegetables and salad dressings.

Rick joined Felicity at the checkout and helped load the groceries into Big Red. As Felicity was putting her bags into the bed of the truck, one of the bags broke, and several cans of vegetables bounced off the bed liner.

"Whoa! Take it easy on Big Red," Rick yelled from the driver side. "Are there any dents? Did you say you're sorry?"

"Sometimes I feel like you love Big Red more than me," Felicity huffed as she slammed her door.

White noise from the hum of the tires on the faded asphalt filled the cab. After several miles passed in silence, Felicity asked, "Rick, who was that guy you were talking to in the grocery store?"

Rick directed his full attention to the road ahead of him, and without looking at Felicity, he responded, "It was Ryan from Lone Star Bank."

"I thought that's who that was. He looked familiar. What did he want?"

"We were just talking business."

"It sounded more like an argument. I'm sure everyone in the store heard you yell that you're not selling. What's going on?"

"It's nothing. Just a little misunderstanding, but he's clear now about what I need."

"Well I'm glad it's clear for someone because I have no idea what's going on. You're stressed out and snapping at people, but you won't tell me why. Is it money? Running the ranch? Is it me?"

"No, it's none of that. I've got everything under control." He flashed a smile he hoped looked reassuring.

Big Red came to a stop in front of the farmhouse, and Rick slammed the truck into park and opened the door in one motion. Felicity grabbed his forearm before he could escape, "Rick, I see you're anxious, and I'd like to help if you'd just let me in on what's going on."

Rick fell back into the driver's seat. "There's nothing to share. Just a lot of long days and hard work to keep this place running. It's stressful at times."

Felicity stared into Rick's eyes. He looked away, and she dropped his arm. She shut the door and leaned in the open window. "I know you're not telling me everything. I have no idea why you can't trust me, but apparently you have everything under control."

Felicity turned toward the farmhouse.

Rick jumped out and yelled over the hood, "Felicity, I didn't say tha—"

Felicity turned around so fast it stopped Rick mid-sentence.

"Rick, you're not the only one who's busy around here. I've got a lot to do before the potluck tomorrow. Bring everything in the house, so I'm not cooking until midnight."

Rick dropped off the last bag of potatoes and shut the pantry door. The secret of the financial condition of FireSky Ranch grew harder to conceal. Could he fix it before Felicity found out?

CHAPTER EIGHT

A rare cold front provided welcome relief to the hot Texas summer. Rick took advantage of the break from the oppressive heat to get in some ground work with a couple of horses before church.

Felicity called out, "Are you ready to go? I don't want to be late. McKenna is coming down for the day and will meet us at church."

Rick and Felicity arrived at Hill Country Community Church and took their usual seats in the third row from the front. A few minutes later, McKenna swept down the aisle in a cobalt blue dress that accented her long, blonde hair. Everyone hugged, and Felicity and McKenna complemented each other on their impeccable fashion sense. The service started and after three worship songs and a prayer, it was time for announcements.

Pastor Scott walked onto the stage in his usual hipster boots and jeans with a classic dress shirt, and invited up a special guest. "Please give Officer Mendoza a warm welcome."

A uniformed officer rose from the front row and joined Pastor Scott onstage, pausing to shake hands.

Pastor Scott moved to the edge of the stage. "Officer Mendoza is here today to share some exciting news about a new program offered by the State of Texas. Government leaders are reaching out to faith communities about participation in this program that is aligned with everything we believe, especially helping neighbors in need. I hope you will all give this program some thoughtful consideration."

Officer Mendoza adjusted his wireless microphone just below his mouth and introduced himself as the community relations director from the Texas Department of Criminal Justice or TDCJ office based in Austin.

"Ladies and gentlemen, I'm here today to share an exciting new program with you. It's called RIHARP. It stands for Residential Inmate Housing and Rehabilitation Program. Like every government program, we have to give it a complicated name, but the concept is simple. RIHARP places individuals incarcerated within the Texas criminal justice system into residential homes to provide those inmates a positive environment for optimal rehabilitation prior to their release. Prisoners will live in the homes of citizens and we hope that many of you will consider hosting some of these inmates."

The congregation of six hundred erupted with groans and a few shouts. It was like a football stadium after a quarterback sack. Officer Mendoza stood silent. As the decibel level lowered, a young lady about halfway back yelled out, "How is that safe?"

"That's a great question and I'm sure one that's on everybody's mind. Let me share more details about the program. RIHARP was tested in the homes of corrections officers, law enforcement, and TDCJ staff for the past three years. RIHARP achieves our high degree of safety from some of the most advanced technology in law enforcement today. It's called Sure Cuffs. The inmates will have tiny rice-sized transmitter chips inserted just under the skin in ten key areas of their bodies."

Officer Mendoza pointed to his wrists, elbows, knees, inner thigh and hips as areas where they have chips implanted.

"It's powered by a quarter-sized device with five years of

battery life. It's inserted just below the hip, and the inmates never feel it after the insertion wound heals."

He pointed to his hip, just below his service belt.

"Sure Cuffs allow the RIHARP inmates to live with host families in a safe environment. Members of the TDCJ staff activated Sure Cuffs dozens of times during the beta-testing phase and it was always successful at subduing the inmate. I've hosted an inmate under the same roof as my wife and two young children. I have complete confidence in Sure Cuffs."

Officer Mendoza moved to the front of the stage where Pastor Scott stood a few minutes earlier.

"Yes, many of the inmates have committed serious and heinous crimes. A judge sentenced all of them to do time in a penitentiary. However, all RIHARP candidates are in the latter half of their sentences and have a sustained record of good behavior. These inmates have been identified through an intense psychological evaluation to have the best opportunity for immersion back into society with the right mentorship and environment."

Officer Mendoza walked to the podium and took a quick drink from his sweaty water glass.

"That's why I'm here today. I'm aware of the reputation of Hill Country Community Church as willing to open your doors to neighbors in need. These inmates are our neighbors. They need to live in a positive environment, so they can make it on the outside once they complete their sentences. RIHARP gives many of them a second chance to be a productive member of society they wouldn't receive without it."

Murmurs broke out in the room again, but Officer Mendoza kept speaking.

"Hosting an inmate comes with financial benefits to offset the care and housing expense of the inmates. So, besides helping an inmate get their life on track, you can also earn a healthy income. If you are interested or have questions, please take a handout in the back when you leave today, and it will have my contact info. Thank you for your time, Hill Country Church!"

Felicity and Rick looked at each other as Officer Mendoza left the stage. Felicity's jaw was open until she whispered, "Wow, I didn't expect to get that message when I walked through the doors today. That's interesting."

Rick kept a watchful eye on Felicity as Pastor Scott continued the service. The bounce in her legs while she sat and her sway when she stood had Rick concerned that Felicity was considering this crazy idea.

McKenna noticed it too, nudging Rick and whispering, "What's with Mom?"

Right after service, the potluck began in the park adjoining the church. Over a hundred families active in the Community Outreach Ministry scattered across picnic tables under grand oak trees to enjoy the spread of food, drinks, and decadent desserts covering three picnic tables. Pastor Scott visited each table to thank them for their service and support of the community. McKenna was updating Rick and Felicity on her summer class and fall schedule at the University of Texas when Pastor Scott arrived at their table.

"Good afternoon, Felicity, Rick, and McKenna. So glad you could celebrate with us on this beautiful, beautiful day. Your service in the Outreach Ministry is genuinely appreciated here at Hill Country Church and everyone it benefits in the community."

"We're happy to help," Felicity responded. "We're ready to pitch in wherever it's needed."

Pastor Scott leaned in as if he would reveal a big secret. "So what did you think about the RIHARP program that Officer Mendoza shared today? I could envision someone living on the Powell ranch and turning their life around."

"It was very interesting," Felicity said with a wide smile.

"It was interesting, but we must discuss it further as a family," Rick interjected.

"I understand. Like I said earlier, I believe RIHARP is a great program and one I hope Christians across Texas and especially here at Hill Country Community Church will embrace. It's a unique opportunity to turn the lives around of people who need it and to model the grace and love of Jesus in our communities. Please reach out to me if you have questions."

As Pastor Scott stepped away, McKenna leaned over the picnic table, "Mom, you're not seriously thinking about doing this, are you?"

"I don't know, honey. Pastor Scott has a good point and—"

McKenna interrupted, "Mom, it's a horrible idea. I don't want a rapist or murderer living in my house. It's not safe for either of you. I'll never visit if you do this crazy program."

"Okay, okay that's enough," Rick interjected. "Nobody has agreed to do anything, and we're not going to discuss it here and now. Let's grab lunch and enjoy this unbelievable cool summer day before McKenna has to go back to campus."

During the drive back to the ranch, the only sound was the crisp Texas air rushing through the open truck windows.

CHAPTER NINE

Rick called Sergio to the porch. He had his laptop open on the wicker table. His eyes flickered each time he toggled the screen.

"Take a look at this, Sergio."

Sergio leaned over to see the screen.

"I'm comparing prices at two different feed and equipment distributors and the price difference on some items can be huge." Rick pointed to his screen, "See this fly mask here? It's twenty-percent cheaper if you buy it from the other guys. Same thing with our brushes, alfalfa seed, and beet pulp pellets for the horses."

Rick leaned back and put his hands in the air, "We can save money if we start buying certain items from this other distributor. What do you think?"

"Of course, saving money is always a good idea, Mr. Powell, but if you don't order enough from either distributor, they may charge you a delivery fee or make you pick everything up. I've compared those two distributors in the past and the extra fees eliminate any savings if you're only buying a few items."

"That's a great point. I hadn't even thought of that, but you're right. I'd get hit with a pretty big delivery fee. Thank you for all your help on everything."

"Your welcome, Mr. Powell."

"Sergio, I've told you a million times before, please call me Rick."

"I'm sorry, but my papa taught me always to be respectful to my employer. I've always been that way."

"That's fine, but you don't have to with me."

"Yes, Mr. Powell."

Rick through his hands in the air, "Come on Sergio, you know —" Rick's cell phone interrupted the exchange. It was Cody and he answered after one ring, "Hey Cody, how's the new job going?"

Cody enthusiastically explained how he enjoyed his new job as an Investment Plan Service Specialist at State Farm Insurance Company. "Dad, I help agents around the country understand and market our financial products. I wouldn't have guessed I'd be doing this after getting a communications degree, but I really like it."

Felicity emerged on the porch.

"Great news, son. It sounds like this new job is a much better fit for you." Rick said as he hit the speaker button on his phone. He held the phone out in front of his body.

"Dad, McKenna called me last night and said you and mom were considering a program at church that would have a prisoner living in our house. Is that true?" Cody's voice crackled through the phone.

Rick glanced at Felicity and laughed.

"No, no, that's not true. They announced a new program like that at church on Sunday, but we haven't talked about it since then. It's not something we'd consider."

"Good. McKenna made it sound like a horrible idea. It concerned me that it was something that y'all were planning to do."

Felicity crossed her arms and leaned against the railing.

"How's everything else going, Dad?"

"Busy as usual. I'll tell you what, I'm here with Sergio and we need to complete our order in the next few minutes, so we can get our feed delivered tomorrow. I'll give the phone to your mom, and I'll call you later when I have more time to talk. Love ya."

Rick handed the phone to Felicity. She turned off the speaker, "Hi, honey, how do you like your new apartment in Dallas?"

The screen door slammed behind her. Rick and Sergio returned their focus to their open order. After they hit submit, Sergio excused himself to tackle his next project in the stables.

Rick went inside and found Felicity standing at the kitchen island.

"How's Cody liking Dallas?"

"Why did you tell him we would never consider the RIHARP program? We haven't even discussed it."

"It sounds like a crazy thing to do. I assumed…"

"I may agree that it sounds crazy, but you can't just make major decisions without discussing them with me. I want to learn more about the program before we say no."

"Seriously? Are you interested just because I assumed you'd agree it was a bad idea?"

"No, I'm interested in helping people turn their lives around. I don't want to sit in my seat every Sunday and listen about how Jesus calls us to love our neighbors and then do nothing. I want to make a difference. I'd like to know if the RIHARP program will allow us to do that. Why can't we at least get more information?"

Rick stood silent. He knew Felicity was right. They should at least investigate a program that can make such a big impact on a person who really needs a helping hand. Plus, she wasn't taking no for an answer.

Rick sighed. "You're right. Pastor Scott seemed excited about the program so let's learn everything we need to know to make a final decision. Together!"

"Thank you. That's all I'm asking."

The next Sunday, the church held an informational meeting on RIHARP for all interested parties. Rick and Felicity left the sanctuary after the noon service and headed into the smaller meeting room with beige patterned carpet and fifteen eight-person round tables and chairs. The smell of burned coffee wafted from the coffee dispensers on the cart pushed against the paneling wall. Only one table was full. Two other couples sat at another table.

Pastor Scott walked into the room and stopped after two steps. "Whoa, I wasn't expecting a full house, but I thought more than this would show up."

"Just the brave few!" joked one of the wives.

Pastor Scott pointed to her, "not only brave, but smart."

Some laughed and others smiled as he moved behind a folding table in the front of the room. He arranged some papers and cleared his throat. "I'm glad y'all have decided to learn more about RIHARP, and hope that you'll come to the same conclusion as me. It's a wonderful way to serve our incarcerated neighbors and change their paths for the better. Let's pray, and I'll get right into sharing more details on RIHARP."

Pastor Scott prayed and then covered the same information as Officer Mendoza had the week before. Rick's mind was elsewhere, and he drew on one of the notepads provided for the table. He drew the layout of the office for JWP group, including a large common area with a ping-pong table, foosball table and a refrigerator stocked with beverages. Rick wrote *Inspiration Room* above the drawing.

"Besides all the benefits of helping these inmates turn their life around, the financial benefits are also attractive."

Rick stopped drawing.

"RIHARP compensation is based on the security level of the inmate. It's $2,000 per month for low security, $3,000 for medium and $4,000 for a maximum-security prisoner."

Now Rick was writing everything down.

Pastor Scott faced Rick and Felicity and took a few steps in their direction, "Rick and Felicity, I know this may be attractive to you. RIHARP inmates can work on host-owned premises with a host present and are paid the same wages for an incarcerated inmate in the State of Texas, which I believe is around fifty cents an hour."

Rick's eyes widened, and he wrote as fast as possible.

Pastor Scott continued with the details. Rick had calculated the financial benefits of each inmate. He concluded that a low-security inmate would provide almost half of his monthly shortfall and be less risky. Besides the wage savings on the inmate, he could also save money on overtime he'd been paying some of the staff the past year.

The meeting ended. During the ride back to FireSky ranch, neither Felicity nor Rick spoke of RIHARP. It was as if they were playing mental poker and neither one wanted to show their hand first.

Rick put the car in park in front of the farmhouse but didn't turn off the engine.

"I've been thinking about the RIHARP program. I'm glad we stayed today to get more information. It's pretty intriguing."

Felicity's face was beaming. "Really? Is it something you'd like to try?"

"I can see all the benefits, and I'm feeling more comfortable with the security measures for a low-security person, but I'm not there yet. It's hard to imagine an inmate living here, on FireSky Ranch, especially after what happened to my dad."

"I understand."

"I need a little more time to wrap my head around all this."

Felicity leaned over and kissed Rick. "Thanks for giving this real consideration. I know how much pain your dad's death caused you. I'll respect whatever you decide. Let's get lunch. I'm starving."

She slid out, then noticed Rick still wearing his seatbelt, both hands on the steering wheel.

"Aren't you coming in?" Felicity asked.

"No, I'm not that hungry. I'll be back in a few hours. I think it's time I paid my mom a visit."

CHAPTER TEN

Rick drove down the tree-lined Austin boulevard until he passed the sign for Gentle Breeze Assisted Care Center. After finding a parking spot, he went inside the sprawling one-story building.

Elizabeth Powell was sitting at a table in the community room watching re-runs. She wore a white button-down blouse with a baby blue sweater draped over her shoulders, an outfit so common for Elizabeth that it could qualify as her official uniform. A deck of perfectly stacked playing cards waited in front of her. The staff had pulled Rick aside during his last visit to tell him Elizabeth was always ready for a game of rummy but had no competitors. She'd developed a reputation as an exceptional card player. The stroke paralyzed her left side and slowed her down in many areas, but rummy was not one.

"Hey, Mom, are you still beating these poor people in rummy every day?" Rick asked as he walked up and planted a kiss on her forehead.

"Theh… Theh… They're all chicken. 'Fraid I'll beat 'em."

They both laughed. Rick joined his mom in watching the next episode of *Everybody Loves Raymond* and brought her up to speed on the grandkids and the ranch.

" Plah…play rummy…with me?"

"Sorry, Mom. Not today, but maybe next time. I'm here because I need your advice on something."

Elizabeth straightened up in her wheelchair. "Wha…Wha… what is it?"

Rick gave her a summary of RIHARP. He included the current financial state of the ranch and the financial benefits for RIHARP hosts. "What do you think?"

"Well, I…don't know. What does Feli…city think?"

"She'd like to give it a shot. We will discuss it later today."

"Wha…Wha…what about you?"

"If you would have asked me yesterday, I would've said I am one-hundred percent against it. Now I'm not so sure what I'd do. It'd be nice to help somebody turn their life around, and the compensation would sure be a welcome addition right now."

Elizabeth did not respond. She fixed her gaze on the scenery outside the large bay window.

"What would Dad do in this situation?"

The right side of Elizabeth's lips curled up.

"That'sss easy. He'd duh…duh…do it."

Rick leaned back and nodded. He'd heard all he needed.

"Thank you, Mom."

Rick returned to FireSky Ranch and searched for Felicity. He found her in the tack room putting away her saddle after an afternoon trail ride.

"How was the ride?" Rick asked.

"It was good. It's nice to get away and soak in the peace and quiet. How was your mom?"

"She's okay. Still kicking everybody's butt in rummy."

Rick leaned against the door frame. He watched Felicity position her saddle next to McKenna's on the second shelf. Felicity adjusted the straps on her saddle when she looked back and saw Rick still standing in the doorway. She stopped, stood up and asked, "Is something wrong?"

Rick smiled, "Let's do it."

That evening, Rick and Felicity gathered around Rick's laptop. They entered all the required information and clicked to the section on the security level of the inmate they wish to host.

"You good with a low-security inmate?" Rick asked as the mouse hovered over the options.

"I'm open." Felicity moved closer to the screen and pointed. "I'd like to help any of them."

Rick bit his lower lip and took a deep breath. "I think I'd feel most comfortable with low-security. "

"That's fine."

Rick chose the low-security inmate option and continued to the end. A "Click to Confirm" button was all that was between them and a submitted RIHARP application.

"You sure about this?"

"I'm sure," Felicity replied without looking away from the screen. She was locked in on submitting the application.

Rick clicked the mouse and yanked his hand up in dramatic fashion. "It's done!"

Over the next two weeks, Rick and Felicity participated in detailed background checks and a half dozen phone screenings with various TDCJ departments. Rick felt like they were defending every decision they'd ever made. One day the call was different. The women on the other end of the call had news to share: "Congratulations. We have accepted your application for a RIHARP inmate."

The next call was from a TDCJ officer with details on the RIHARP inmate transition plan. He shared that their inmate would be assigned soon and they'd receive a letter in the mail from TDCJ with their inmate's profile. The final step of the transition plan would occur on drop off day with detailed training and set up with their new inmate.

Felicity checked the mailbox every day right after the mail carrier left. Two weeks after the onboarding transition call, an official-looking letter arrived with a return address of the Texas Department of Criminal Justice in Austin.

She rushed inside and said, "I think this is it."

Rick was standing in front of the open refrigerator contemplating snack choices. He closed it and said, "Open her up. Let's see who we've got."

Felicity tore open the envelope and unfolded the letter.

After a minute she looked up and smiled. "His name is Jeff Stratton."

The letter included a one-page profile on the inmate with general information like his age, birth date, hometown, and date he entered the TDCJ system. Jeff was a low-security inmate from Ruben M. Torres Unit Texas state prison in Medina County, Texas.

Rick read the letter. "It says we'll receive a comprehensive RIHARP inmate profile 'upon delivery' of the inmate. It feels like we just ordered a supreme pizza, hot wings, and a side of low-security prisoner. Hold the mushrooms but give me some extra felony charges."

Rick laughed at his own joke, but Felicity didn't look up from the letter.

"I can't wait to meet him," she said as she reread the letter a third time.

Like expectant parents, Rick and Felicity prepared the first-floor bedroom suite for Jeff. After Rick finished changing the sheets and replacing the pillows on the bed, he picked up a picture from the dresser. It was a photo of Elizabeth standing next to a bay horse with a braided black mane after a ride on FireSky Ranch when her father-in-law was still alive. This had been her room for over twenty years. Rick scanned the room and put the picture on a bookcase opposite the bed, so Mom could keep an eye on this guy.

He lay on the bed, facing the ceiling, and wondered if he was making a mistake.

CHAPTER ELEVEN

Thick gray clouds choked out the sun. The humidity was so thick it required extra effort to take each breath. Rick and Felicity finished dinner and then loitered on the porch as they waited for their new RIHARP house guest. They both moved to the railing when two black GMC Yukon SUVs pulled into the driveway.

Three TDCJ corrections officers emerged. Officer Mendoza, the speaker who'd announced RIHARP Hill Country Church, was one. He greeted Rick and Felicity at the end of the sidewalk while the other two stood by the rear passenger door. Officer Mendoza extended his hand to Rick and Felicity.

"Hello Mr. and Mrs. Powell, it's a pleasure to see you again. I'll be guiding you through the exchange process today."

He opened his arms and asked, "Are you ready to meet your RIHARP inmate?"

Rick froze. His eyes locked on the passenger door.

Felicity bounced on her toes with her hands in prayer position in front of her lips. "Yes," she responded.

Officer Mendoza turned around and nodded to the officers.

The door opened. Wavy blond hair emerged first. Then the rest of his slender six-foot-two-inch frame appeared in an orange jumpsuit.

Rick exhaled. He was expecting to see a hardened criminal with face and neck tattoos. Instead, the young man looked like a lost surfer.

Rick caught a quick smile from Felicity.

When Jeff reached the sidewalk, there was an awkward silence until Officer Mendoza spoke. "Mr. and Mrs. Powell, this is Jeff Stratton and he will be in your custody today."

Jeff extended his hand with a bright smile. "Hello, Mr. Powell, it's a pleasure to meet you."

Rocky growled as they shook hands.

"Rocky, no," Rick commanded. "I'm sorry, he doesn't normally do that. He needs to get used to you."

Jeff took a step back. "Good looking dog, Mr. Powell. Is he a German Shepherd?"

"He's a Belgian Malinois. He's a great dog."

The transition from ranch owners to RIHARP wardens continued inside the farmhouse.

Officer Mendoza prepared the RIHARP instructions and requirements for Rick and Felicity. The other officers took Jeff to audit the GPS settings at the FireSky property boundaries. They also tested the elevation boundary of the second story with the inmate.

Officer Mendoza sat down, and Rick and Felicity sat across from him around the dining room table that once hosted dinners for Grandpa Powell and his family. Officer Mendoza had a three-inch binder with colorful flyers and pamphlets. He removed a small stack of papers from his binder and began, "Mr. and Mrs. Powell, I'm here today to give you all the details on hosting an inmate through the RIHARP program, including your requirements."

Officer Mendoza outlined the required living arrangements, reporting parameters, and legal liabilities.

"Next, I'll cover the part that allows inmates to live in a residential home with citizen hosts, Sure Cuffs." Officer Mendoza slid a brochure on Sure Cuffs across the table to Rick and Felicity.

"I realize you've heard of this a few times already, but it's important for your safety that you understand everything about this technology."

He stood up to demonstrate.

"You might recall my descriptions of Sure Cuffs. It works by inserting ten rice-sized transmitter chips under the skin of each RIHARP inmate. They're located on each side in their inner knee, thigh, upper hip area, elbow and in the palm of their hand near their thumbs."

Officer Mendoza turned his hand around and ran his other index finger down until he came to the base of his thumb in the palm of his hand. "It's placed right about here."

"This placement is important because these ten chips, when activated, secure the inmate's knees together while bringing their arms and hands in tight next to their body, almost like a soldier standing at attention. In this position, it immobilizes the inmate, and he will often fall to the ground. The inmates will remain in this position until Sure Cuffs are deactivated on your smartphone app or by a TDCJ officer. The app notifies our office when Sure Cuffs are activated, and we'll dispatch local authorities and TDCJ officers to investigate. Sometimes an officer from the Office of the Inspector General may also investigate."

Officer Mendoza pointed to the brochure he'd given them.

"Sure Cuffs are tested multiple times with each inmate as a precursor to their acceptance into the RIHARP program. We need to verify it works on the inmate and the inmates need to know the effectiveness of Sure Cuffs. It's a good deterrent to any potential confrontations. Inmates are not in pain after Sure Cuffs are activated, but they are uncomfortable and can get hurt if they fall. Plus, several law enforcement agencies show up to investigate every activation of Sure Cuffs, as I mentioned, so activate wisely."

Felicity and Rick leaned toward Officer Mendoza with wide eyes.

Officer Mendoza took a drink of water and continued, "There are several ways to activate Sure Cuffs. One is via GPS boundaries. This includes elevation changes like the second story of your home or a barn. The other officers are calibrating and validating those precise locations right now. If the inmate crosses the GPS boundaries, Sure Cuffs will activate, and we'll come to pick him up. He'll serve the rest of his sentence behind bars. You chose when to activate the other three options."

Officer Mendoza held up three fingers. "Those three options are your smartphone app, an emergency word, and a loud noise like a clap or a yell in proximity to the inmate."

Officer Mendoza clapped, and Rocky jumped up from his afternoon nap.

"Now, we need to establish an emergency activation word. Think of a single word that is not something you'd say in a normal course of your day, but you'll remember under stress or in an emergency."

Felicity and Rick looked around the room for inspiration. After a minute, Rick jumped up in excitement like a grade school boy with the right answer. "I know what we can use as our word! Wookie."

"Rookie?" Officer Mendoza asked.

"No, wookie. Chewbacca in Star Wars is a wookie."

"Oh, yeah." Officer Mendoza smiled. "The big furry guy. I like it."

Felicity shook her head at Rick and Officer Mendoza had their moment. "Star Wars. Really?"

Officer Mendoza composed himself and continued, "I've covered everything I have to share on Sure Cuffs. I'll give you two a few minutes to review the rest of the brochure. Let me know if you have questions."

Officer Mendoza excused himself to check on the other officers while Rick and Felicity read the rest of the pamphlet.

Five minutes later, Officer Mendoza returned and Felicity said, "I have a question."

"Yes, ma'am."

"I see that it discourages certain activities like swimming and horseback riding. Why is that?"

"Great question, Mrs. Powell. It's because once Sure Cuffs are activated, the inmate cannot move or defend themselves. If they're swimming and Sure Cuffs is activated, they could drown. Riding a horse could endanger both the horse and the inmate."

"Unless GPS activates it, don't we decide when Sure Cuffs gets activated?" Felicity inquired.

"In theory, yes, but remember a loud noise can also activate Sure Cuffs. A shotgun blast, a clap of thunder, a smoke alarm and several other unintentional loud noises could activate Sure Cuffs."

"I hadn't even thought of that. It makes sense now."

"That brings me to my next request. I'll need a safety word to deactivate Sure Cuffs if they activate at a time that puts the inmate in danger. The word will deactivate Sure Cuffs for two minutes to remove the inmate from a dangerous situation. The safety word can be used twice per hour before it requires the smartphone app to deactivate Smart Cuffs permanently."

"Wow, you guys have thought of everything," Felicity exclaimed.

"We've had to add a lot of these features after something happened during the beta phase."

Felicity smiled at Rick. "I get to pick this time."

She stood, and paced next to the table, looking out the window, and then she spun around. "Let's go with Atticus. It's for Atticus Finch in my all-time favorite book *To Kill a Mockingbird*."

"Great choice, Mrs. Powell," Officer Mendoza replied as he jotted it down in his notes. "The other officers will get those set up as soon as they return from the GPS validation."

Officer Mendoza answered several more questions from Felicity.

Felicity turned to Rick. "You've been quiet. I've been asking all the questions. Do you have any questions for Officer Mendoza while he is here?"

Rick furrowed his brow and pinched his lips. "Yeah, are Sure Cuffs one-hundred percent effective at keeping us safe?"

Officer Mendoza placed his hat on the table. "Sir, not much in this world is one-hundred percent. But this technology was for me. I had an inmate in my house for eighteen months with my wife and two young kids, both under ten years old. My wife was a nervous wreck when he arrived. He's a former gang member from Houston in prison for multiple murders. At the end of the beta test, my wife didn't want him to leave. So yeah, I expect Sure Cuffs will keep you and your family safe."

Officer Mendoza left the kitchen and returned with a woman in her mid-forties. Her professional attire complemented her disarming smile. They both sat down at the kitchen table opposite Rick and Felicity.

"Now I want to introduce you to the TDCJ health specialist assigned to this RIHARP case. Mrs. Sawyer is available to the inmate and RIHARP hosts."

She walked around the table and shook hands with Felicity and then Rick.

"Hi, I'm Kimberly Sawyer. It's nice to meet both of you." Her voice was as soft as her handshake. Mrs. Sawyer returned to her seat beside Officer Mendoza.

"Allowing an inmate in your home is a big transition, and you will run into situations that nobody else will understand. I'm here to help you get through everything, including any personal issues that may arise because of RIHARP. My goal as a TDCJ health specialist is to help inmates optimize their rehabilitation experience and their eventual transition to civilian life."

Felicity exhaled and sunk back into her chair.

Mrs. Sawyer reached out and patted Felicity's hands resting on the table. "I'm here for you. You won't go through any of this alone."

"Thank you, Mrs. Sawyer."

Mrs. Sawyer opened a manila folder. After reviewing it for a couple of seconds, she continued, "although the inmates are out of prison, which may seem like a vacation to you and me, it's a big change for them, and they may need time to adjust. The world has changed a lot since they were last free and it comes at them very fast. It's not uncommon for some of them to have mood swings or develop depression as they try to cope with their new life on the other side of the bars. It's important for us to communicate and for you to contact me if you have questions."

Felicity and Rick looked at each other and Felicity responded, "Okay, we'll call you if we have questions or concerns."

Officer Mendoza rose from his chair and said, "Okay, you're ready now."

He pushed toward them a large binder labeled "RIHARP Inmate Profile: Jeffery Stratton."

"This binder contains all the information on Mr. Stratton. It contains his personal history and his psychological profile. I'd recommend reading this information as soon as possible so you are aware of his background, habits, and everything else that can help make hosting him a smooth transition."

"The last thing we need to do is to verify Sure Cuffs. As soon as Officer Tellez returns from the GPS boundary test with Mr. Stratton, we'll have you test the app and emergency word."

Moments later, the two officers returned with Jeff and everyone assembled in the family room.

"Time to test Sure Cuffs. Mr. Powell, please active the app on your phone."

Rick looked down at his phone and up at the inmate standing in the middle of his family room—the same room where he remembered wrestling on the floor with his dad forty years ago. Rick hit the oversized green button on his screen that said "Activate," and Jeff's legs and arms snapped to his sides. He looked like a soldier standing at attention with a slight lean forward and stiffness that made him wobble in the middle of the room.

"Great. See how that works Mr. Powell? Go ahead and hit the red 'Deactivate' button."

Jeff's arms and legs loosened from his body. He shook out each arm and leg and rotated his neck.

"Okay, Mrs. Powell, please activate Sure Cuffs with the emergency word."

Felicity looked at Jeff, paused and whispered, "wookie."

Nothing happened.

"Say it like you mean it, Mrs. Powell." Officer Mendoza barked. "Remember, this is the word to secure Mr. Stratton in an instant during an emergency."

Felicity cleared her throat and shouted "wookie!"

Jeff snapped back in a subdued position. He clenched his jaw and glared at Felicity.

"Thata girl," Officer Mendoza said with a toothy grin.

"I'm sorry, Jeff. Are you all right?" Felicity asked.

"Never been better," Jeff snarled through gritted teeth.

Rick turned to see Felicity's reaction. He put his hands in his pockets and took a long look at Jeff out of the corner of his eye. Jeff's glare was something Rick would not soon forget.

"Mrs. Powell, please deactivate Sure Cuffs on your phone."

The officers completed their RIHARP transition checklist.

"Goodbye, Mr. and Mrs. Powell," Officer Mendoza and Mrs. Sawyer said in unison as they waved and exited the house.

Rick, Felicity, and Jeff stood in awkward silence in the family room. Rick cleared his throat and asked, "Jeff, would you like a tour of the place?"

"Sure."

First, Rick gave Jeff a tour of the first floor of the farmhouse. Then he directed Jeff to the guest suite.

"The folks at RIHARP gave us your sizes, so we have regular clothes for you in the dresser and closet. The remote for the TV is on the nightstand and towels are under the sink in the bathroom if you want to take a shower."

Jeff sat on the bed and scanned the room.

"Thanks, Rick."

"I prefer Mr. Powell for now."

"Got it, Mr. Powell."

"I'll show you the rest of the ranch when it's light out tomorrow. We've all had a long day, so I'll leave you to get settled in your room and see you in the morning."

Rick passed Rocky laying down in the kitchen. He was laser-focused on the closed guest room door down the hall.

"Good boy," Rick said as he gave Rocky few pats on his head and proceeded to his bedroom upstairs.

Felicity was reading Jeff's profile binder in bed.

"Did you know he's doing nine years for a strong-arm robbery and assault? He threatened to kill the female clerk if she didn't give him the money. He denied it, but the security footage backed up the clerk's story. Plus, the clerk and some witnesses testified that they felt he was serious about killing her if she didn't give him the money. He has four more years left in his sentence. I'd never have guessed he was in prison. He looks like such a nice boy."

"He's a convicted felon. We have to be careful no matter how harmless or nice he looks."

"Rick, someday you will learn to trust people."

"Maybe, but I saw the look on his face when you activated Sure Cuffs. If looks could kill, you'd be in trouble right now."

CHAPTER TWELVE

Rick shuffled into the kitchen and jumped when he looked over to the kitchen table.

"Sorry Jeff, I'm not used to seeing anybody else up at this time. Is everything okay?"

"Yeah, everything is fine. It's so quiet here. I need to get used to it."

"Help yourself to some coffee, eggs and bacon from the refrigerator, or whatever you'd like for breakfast. I need to check on a pregnant mare, so I'll be back soon."

Rick returned a few hours later. Jeff was in his room with the door shut and Felicity was in the kitchen. Her cheeks had evidence of dried tears.

"What's wrong?"

"Can we go outside on the porch to talk?" Felicity was already moving toward the front door.

Rick picked up his pace and felt a bolt of heat rush up his back. "Did Jeff do something?"

"No, it's not Jeff. It's Cody and McKenna. I told them we have a RIHARP inmate living on the ranch and they got nasty with me. Cody was in disbelief. He kept saying 'That's crazy' and 'I can't believe you and dad would do something that dumb.' McKenna was angry. She yelled that we were putting everyone in danger and hung up on me."

"I'm sorry, honey. It may take everyone a while to come around. RIHARP is a polarizing program. Some people may never support our decision."

Tears welled up and ran down Felicity's cheeks. "I didn't expect Cody and McKenna to be so angry. I'm just trying to help someone turn his life around. I was hoping for a little more support."

"Give them a little time. They understand deep down that you're only trying to help like you always do, so give them some time to process it. I'll call them in a couple of days and see if they are coming around."

After lunch, Rick took Jeff on a tour of FireSky Ranch and walked him through every stable. He introduced Jeff to Sergio and his staff.

As Jeff was shaking hands and introducing himself to the rest of the team, Sergio told Rick, "I was expecting a really bad guy. He doesn't seem so bad."

"My first impression is good so let's put him to work right away and see what he's made of."

Sergio assigned stall cleanup to Jeff. The rest of the crew welcomed the new addition at the bottom of the pecking order.

While Rick was loading forty-pound bags into the bed of Big Red at the feed store, Mark Cochran from Circle G, a neighboring ranch, confronted him in the parking lot.

"Hey Rick, what's this I hear about a prisoner living on your ranch?"

"His name is Jeff and he'll be staying with us for a while."

"Is that legal?" Mark asked.

"It's a program through the state of Texas, so I reckon it is."

"Seems like you're putting a lot of innocent people at risk by keeping a prisoner so close to our homes," Mark sneered.

"Don't worry, he can't leave our property. It's kinda like house arrest and seems safe so far."

"Well, I don't like it. Keep him away from my ranch. If I see an inmate poking around on my property, I'll have no choice but to defend my family and me."

"Duly noted. I won't bring him by for trick or treating this year."

"I can't believe Felicity ever let you pull a stunt like this. What was she thinking?"

"It was her idea."

Mark clenched his jaw and his nostrils flared. Rick cracked a smile when he observed Mark trying to speak, but no sound coming out.

"I'd love to chat more about your fear of anyone new in this neighborhood, but I've got several more bags of feed to load. You lookin' to help?" Rick asked as he bent over and grabbed another bag.

"Just keep your prisoner away from our ranch!" Mark said and stormed away.

"That went well."

After leaving the feed store, Rick's phone blasted a ring tone he didn't hear often. It was his brother. Rick considered letting it go to voicemail, but instead answered. "What's up, Jack?"

Jack's deep voice filled Big Red through the radio speakers. "What's going on down there, Rick? A prisoner living on our ranch? Are you going crazy?"

"Not today, Jack. I got grilled by Mark from Circle G two minutes ago."

"Well, what did you tell him? I'm dying to hear what you're thinking."

Rick paused as he turned down the blacktop road toward FireSky Ranch. Once he chose the right words, he replied, "It's a great way to put an inmate in a positive environment so they have a better chance of making it on the outside once released. It's safe, we get cheap labor on the ranch, and the pay doesn't hurt. Plus,

Mom said it sounded like a program Dad would have supported."

Jack was silent.

Rick wasn't sure if he lost the connection. "Are you still there?"

"Yeah, I'm still here. I'm just trying to imagine running a ranch and equestrian training facility while an inmate is living with me and my family. It sounds like an awful lot to take on."

Rick rolled his eyes and shook his head. "It is a lot, but I've got this."

"I hope so."

"Look, Jack I'm about to pull into FireSky, and I have some hungry horses that need to get fed," Rick shared.

"Speaking of FireSky, how is the ranch? Cassie is concerned you are struggling with the business side. Should I come down to make sure everything is running okay?"

Oh great. Jack's trying to swoop into FireSky Ranch to save the day. I'm surprised it took this long to try.

Rick suppressed saying what was really on his mind and replied, "That won't be necessary. Everything is fine and Cassie needs to stop worrying so much. It's a lot of work, but I've got it under control."

Jack was silent again on the other end for a few seconds.

"Do you need money? I have a little savings I could donate to the cause."

It was Rick's turn for silence. He considered it for a nanosecond. It would make life a little easier.

"I'd hate for you to have to fill the place with prisoners to make ends meet," Jack added.

Nope, Jack would belittle every decision I made, change everything, and then fly home. leaving me to deal with the consequences. No amount of money was worth it.

"Nah, I'm good. Thanks for the offer, though."

After the sun fell below the horizon and the stars appeared, Rick started a fire in the backyard. Felicity joined him. They talked about all the opposition to Jeff from friends, family, and neighbors.

Rick said, "I know it's tough having everyone against this, but they don't understand how much we are helping someone like Jeff. Plus, the extra money will sure be a nice addition. I'm sure they'll come around."

Felicity leaned her head on Rick's shoulder. "I sure hope so."

CHAPTER THIRTEEN

Sergio taught Jeff how to transfer alfalfa hay from the barn to the stables. Rick stopped by the stables and saw Jeff moving back and forth with a purpose. Sweat bled through the back of his shirt.

Rick found Sergio in the round pen. "How's Jeff working out?"

Sergio walked over to the fence and leaned on the top rail. "So far so good."

"He seems like a hard worker."

"Yeah, he's always on his best behavior around me, but a few of the guys complained he likes to mix it up when I'm not around."

Rick put his foot on the first rung of the fence and leaned on the top rail next to Sergio. "What do you mean?"

"I guess he likes to talk smack. Nothing the crew doesn't already do with each other, but it seems a little early for him."

"Hmmm," Rick responded and watched Jeff dart between stables.

After the sun dropped below the canopy of trees, Rick, Felicity, and Jeff sat down together for dinner. Jeff was more talkative than normal. He shared how hot it was in the barn. Rick countered with several stories justifying his disdain for barn work in summer. The stories halted and eating sped up once Felicity unveiled her mouthwatering feast. Fresh-cut, seasoned potato wedges, jalapeno cornbread, and buttered sweet corn, accompanied the main event — slow-roasted beef ribs.

When they finished eating, Felicity excused herself and put her plate of rib bones on the counter. Jeff did the same but did not push his plate onto the counter far enough and it crashed to the floor. The plate broke into dozens of pieces and rib bones flew everywhere.

Jeff froze. Seconds later he dropped to the floor and hurried to pick up pieces of the broken plate. Felicity turned around and bent down to pick up the bones.

"I've got it," Jeff said as he methodically picked up a piece every few seconds.

Felicity increased her pace. More bones and pieces of the plate were on her plate. "I'm just trying to hurry and get this before—"

"I said I've got this!" Jeff barked.

Felicity jerked back into the cabinets below the sink so fast she ended up in a seated position.

"Watch your tone!" Rick thundered as he stood up behind the table.

Jeff stood up with a puzzled look. He crossed his arms, then interlocked his hands at his waist and settled leaving his hands in his pockets.

"I'm sorry, Mr. Powell."

"Don't apologize to me. You yelled at Mrs. Powell, and that's not okay."

Jeff looked over at Felicity. She rose from the floor and stood with a plate full of bones and plate shards.

Jeff opened his mouth to talk and stopped twice before he muttered, "I'm sorry, Mrs. Powell. In prison, dropping something in the dining hall attracts attention. Unwanted attention. The guards and inmates give you a hard time if you attract any attention to yourself. I guess it still stresses me out."

"None of that will happen to you here, Jeff," Felicity said in a steady, quiet voice.

"I know. It's just hard to get out of my head after so long. I'm sorry about the mess."

"Get cleaned up for the night. You've had a long day. I'll finish this."

"Thanks, Mrs. Powell."

Rick kept his eyes on Jeff until he reached his room and shut the door.

"Are you okay?"

"I'm fine. He caught me off guard. I feel terrible that he still feels so stressed about dropping a plate. That must be awful."

"I didn't expect that kind of reaction, either. He worked hard today. Maybe he's tired." Rick pushed his plate to the back of the counter. He grabbed a sponge and turned on the hot water. "This is new for everyone, so we need to be careful with him."

"I will. I still feel bad for him," Felicity replied.

Rick finished with the dishes and grabbed a lighter from the junk drawer.

Felicity asked, "You going to sit by the fire tonight?"

"Yeah, I'll have it roaring in a few minutes."

Once Felicity finished cleaning up, she joined Rick by the fire pit. He slumped in his chair, holding his old baseball glove.

"Is everything okay?"

"Yeah, just thinking." Rick's voice cracked.

Felicity dragged her chair next to Rick's until they were touching. "What is it?"

Rick shook his head. He turned to Felicity and opened his mouth. Nothing came out. He looked down, up at the sky, and then at his hands.

"Why do these guys get a second chance? My dad didn't get one. He's dead, and the guy who killed him should've still been in prison that day."

Rick bent over and tossed a small branch on the fire. "They let him out early to save a few bucks. For 'good behavior' is what they said. So what's a guy do that already has three DUI's? He gets hammered and blows a stop sign going sixty-five and T-bones my dad. The Coroner said Dad never had a chance. I've been serving my thirty-two-year sentence without him ever since."

Rick could recall every detail after the sheriff's officers knocked on their front door. It was as vivid as if it happened yesterday. His mom collapsed when she heard the news. Moments before, she'd been hopping mad because Big Jack was supposed to pick up Rick after his baseball game and didn't show up. Rick was holding his baseball glove waiting to tell his dad about his two doubles and a single that day.

Rick looked down at the glove on his lap and his eyes filled with tears.

"I don't get it. Someone like Jeff gets the chance of a lifetime to get out of prison early and live with on this beautiful ranch and my dad is gone forever. It doesn't seem fair."

Felicity held Rick's free hand between hers.

"It's hard to give someone a second chance when they act so ungrateful," Rick continued. "I wanted to throw Jeff through a wall when he snapped at you. I don't get our justice system. I've been wondering why any inmate should get an opportunity like this. Does any of what I'm saying make sense to you?"

"Yes, it does," Felicity whispered. "Let's give this one a chance and see how it goes."

Rick turned toward the flickering flames and nodded.

Together, they watched two more logs burn without uttering another syllable.

Over the next month, the Powells extended their ranch's hospitality to their RIHARP inmate. The first RIHARP check was scheduled to arrive soon. Rick checked the stack of mail every day looking for the TDCJ return address. Under an envelope promising zero interest on a balance transfer to a new credit card, he saw TDCJ on West Fourteenth Street in Austin, Texas as the return address. He tore it open. It was the biggest two-thousand dollar check he'd ever seen.

He found Sergio. "Let's order that pump we need to keep the pond full at the south end."

"I thought that project was on hold until we get a few more leases."

"The pond is drying up, so we need to do something, or we won't be able to let the herd graze in the south end anymore. It'll cost us more in hay in the long-run if we don't keep that pond full. Plus, I got my first check from the state for hosting Jeff."

"Great news, Mr. Powell. I'll order it today."

Later that week, Rick and Felicity were reclining in the shade of their porch. A breeze made the summer evening tolerable. They waved to Sergio as he put his bag in the truck's bed and climbed in the cab.

A white delivery truck kicked up dust as it rumbled toward the house.

"That's your pump, Mr. Powell," Sergio yelled from his truck.

The delivery driver slid the box onto the lift gate and lowered it.

"Wow, that's bigger than I was expecting," Rick said.

"Do you want to get it going tonight?" Sergio inquired.

"No, we can do it tomorrow."

"I won't be here. Anna has her appointment with the specialist in Austin, and it will take several hours. I won't be back until Monday."

"No, no Sergio. That's right. Go take care of Anna, and I'll get this going myself."

"Mr. Powell, that's a two-person job. I'd rather stay late tonight and get that done."

Rick looked at Felicity, and she shrugged. He looked to the west.

"It looks like we still have an hour of daylight so let's do it."

Felicity leaned back and closed her eyes. The wind chimes played a steady melody. After twenty minutes passed, she went inside and found Jeff rooting around in the freezer.

"Whatcha looking for?"

"I'm still hungry. I thought I saw a slice of pizza in here."

"Pull out the bottom shelf. It's underneath the frozen cauliflower," Felicity said, pointing to the shelf.

Jeff found the pizza and put it in the toaster oven.

"I'd be faster if you nuked it for a few seconds."

"Nah, it gets too soggy."

"Just be careful, that toaster is on the fritz," Felicity cautioned. "One coil gets extra hot, and it's easy to burn stuff. I'm fixin' to get a new one soon."

"No problem."

Felicity left the kitchen. She curled up on the couch with her laptop in the family room. She smelled something burning and rushed into the kitchen. Smoke was billowing out of the toaster oven. The pizza was on fire.

"Oh my gosh," Felicity said as she sprinted toward the toaster oven.

Jeff came out of his room. "What the…?"

"It's on fire!" Felicity yelled.

Jeff sprinted over to Felicity.

"I'll get it."

Before Jeff could move, Felicity turned off the toaster and stabbed the pizza with a long barbeque fork.

"I said, I'll get it," Jeff protested.

Felicity was a dozen steps ahead of him and out the front door with the smoking pizza on a fork. She galloped down the patio steps and continued another twenty paces from the farmhouse, out by Rocky's doghouse. She dropped the fork with the pizza into his water dish, and it smoldered.

The screen door slammed. Felicity looked up and saw Jeff charging down the steps toward her. His eyes were small, and cheeks flushed.

"I told you I would get it!" Jeff shouted.

Felicity turned to face Jeff as he closed the distance between them.

"What's wrong with you, woman? When I say I'll get it, I mean I'll get it!"

He was ten feet from Felicity, and his pace was accelerating.

"Wookie!"

Jeff's arms and legs snapped together as Sure Cuffs activated. He fell face-first into the grass.

Neither moved for the two seconds that felt like an hour after Jeff hit the turf. He was shouting into the grass, but Felicity couldn't make out all the words. She recognized a few from the times her dad hit his finger with a hammer.

Felicity ran into the house and found her cell phone charging on the counter. Jeff stopped yelling, and Felicity kneeled next to him.

"I'm sorry, Jeff. You seemed so angry, and I wasn't sure you would stop."

"I wouldn't hurt you. I was just mad." Jeff's voice was muffled by the grass.

"Fair enough. I'll deactivate the Sure Cuffs, and I need you to walk straight into the house. Once you're inside, stay in your room for the rest of the night or I'll activate them again."

Jeff didn't respond.

"Did you hear me?"

"Fine, just hurry and let me get off this grass."

Felicity took a few steps back. She hit "Deactivate" on her phone and looked to Jeff. He got up got up on one knee and brushed grass clippings off his T-shirt. He stood and wiped off his blue jeans. Felicity took another step back, her finger an inch above the "Activate" button. Jeff glared at Felicity and then turned toward the house. He walked up the stairs with a slight limp until he vanished behind the front door.

Felicity texted Rick: *Come home ASAP.*

CHAPTER FOURTEEN

R ick and Sergio skidded to a stop in front of the farmhouse twenty minutes later. They parked next to a black Ford Explorer SUV with a white sheriff decal on the side.

Rick saw Felicity talking to a woman in a sheriff's department uniform at the bottom of the porch steps. Rick darted up the sidewalk and gave Felicity a side hug.

"Are you okay?"

"I am now. Just a little shaken."

"What happened? Where's Jeff?" Rick asked, looking around.

"Jeff's inside for the night. I was just telling the deputy about what happened."

Felicity recapped the scene for Rick and the deputy.

After Felicity finished, the deputy said, "Thank you, ma'am. I will take Mr. Stratton's statement now."

Once the deputy had her directions to Jeff's room and left to get his statement, Rick asked, "Why do you think he got so upset over burned pizza?"

"I don't know. It came out of left field, and that's what made it so scary. He was fine one second and then raging the next."

"You didn't do anything else that you didn't tell the deputy, did you?"

"What do you mean? Are you asking if I did some to provoke him?" Felicity snapped, her voice a couple of octaves higher.

"No, I'm just confused why he would act that way. He's been working with us on the ranch for a couple of months now, and I've never seen him act like that. I'm just trying to figure out what set him off."

"Well, I can assure you it had nothing to do with me. I can't believe you think I provoked him." Felicity stormed off the porch and into the house.

Rick followed her. "That's not what I'm trying to—"

But Felicity was already up the stairs.

Rick saw the deputy shutting the door to Jeff's room. She motioned for Rick to follow her as she walked outside to the porch.

"Where's Mrs. Powell?"

"She's upset, so she went up to the bedroom."

"Hmm. Okay," the deputy responded as she studied Rick's facial expression a little longer than he expected.

"Have you reviewed Mr. Stratton's entire file?"

Shaking his head, Rick replied, "No, I haven't, but I think Felicity has."

"I'd advise both of you to take a deep look at it together. It may explain why he's acting this way toward your wife. I've seen guys like him before."

"What is it? What should we be looking for?" Rick asked.

"I can't say for sure because I haven't seen the file myself, but he was short with me during my investigation, and it sounds like he's okay with you."

Rick furrowed his brow and stroked his goatee with his thumb and index finger.

"I'm done here, Mr. Powell, so please review that file."

Rick dug through the desk in the hallway until he found Jeff's background file from the full RIHARP packet. He committed to reading Jeff's entire file to see if he could find what the deputy suggested may trigger Jeff. Rick read about many troubling events in Jeff's past, including some time in foster care. The clock in the kitchen chimed twice before Rick went to bed.

The next day Rick and Jeff spent the day working on the ranch. Their conversations were short and light. He couldn't get Jeff's troubled past out of his mind.

Rick and Jeff arrived back at the farmhouse for dinner. Except for the clinking of knives and forks on the porcelain plates, dinner was silent. After dinner, Rick found Felicity on the porch. She was pushing herself in the swing with one foot while the other leg curled beneath her.

As soon as Rick sat down, a maroon Ford Taurus pulled into the parking area between the house and the stables. Rocky charged toward the vehicle and barked to make his presence known. The passenger window rolled down, and Rick bent down from his seat to see inside. It was Mrs. Sawyer.

"Rocky, on the porch."

Rocky retreated. Rick met Mrs. Sawyer at the end of the sidewalk. She had a large bag over her shoulder and was carrying a leather-bound portfolio.

Rick extended his arms. "Here, let me get that for you."

They marched up the stairs and met Felicity on the porch.

"I'm sure you're here because of the incident."

"I wanted to see how you're doing. How *are* you doing Mrs. Powell?"

"A little better today."

"Good. I'd also like to talk to Mr. Stratton. Would that be okay?"

"Sure, he's in the guest suite just down the hall from the kitchen."

"Thank you, Mrs. Powell. I'll be back soon."

Rick and Felicity waited on the porch. As the orange sun turned into a half circle behind the pasture in the west, Mrs. Sawyer emerged from the house.

"Is it okay to talk out here?"

"Sure."

"Why don't you both come a little closer so we can discuss what I've found with Jeff."

Rick moved to a chair next to the wicker couch where Mrs. Sawyer sat beside Felicity.

"Before we get started, would you like something to drink?" Felicity offered.

"No thank you, Mrs. Powell, I'm great right now."

She opened her leather portfolio on the wicker coffee table. It had two pages of notes.

"I found information on Jeff that may explain why he is acting out toward you."

"So, it's not because I provoked him?" Felicity grumbled while flashing Rick a side eye.

"Oh no, Mrs. Powell, it has nothing to do with you. It has to do with the emotional baggage Jeff has been carrying."

Mrs. Sawyer glanced at her notes, then turned toward Felicity.

"When Jeff was eleven, the Texas Department of Family and Protective Services took him away from his mother while they investigated her for child abuse. He lived with his grandmother during this investigation. Six months later, they accused her of abusing him as well. They placed Jeff with his uncle until he was sixteen and then he moved back with his mom. The police were called to their house twice by neighbors for fighting before Jeff moved out when he was eighteen. Jeff seemed to be staying out of trouble until the strong-arm robbery that put him in prison."

"I read all that. How does that explain why he seems to have a problem with me?" Felicity asked as she wiped away a tear that made it to her lips.

"I see this among many of the male inmates. They're abused by women—mothers, aunts, or grandmothers—while they are young. This leads to a defensive position against anyone of that gender. If they feel threatened by a woman, they lash out. Some of those men learn that it was an individual who hurt them, and they grow to have healthy relationships with women. Others foster too much anger and bitterness toward women, and it leads to a lifetime of physical abuse."

Rick leaned in. "Which one is Jeff?"

"I'm not sure yet. That's what I'm here to investigate. How does he act toward you Mr. Powell?"

"He's respectful. I haven't had any issues with him, but I see how he looks at Felicity, and it concerns me."

Mrs. Sawyer jotted down more notes. "Hmm. Okay, thank you."

She turned back to Felicity. "You're a kind woman, but you are also a strong woman, and that may trigger something in him. The deputy said in her notes he was short with her, too."

Felicity turned to catch the tip of the sun descending below the horizon. She exhaled and leaned back into the cushions.

"That makes sense. He gets irritated so fast when I ask him to do anything."

Rick added, "It's not you, honey. It's his past, and he seems scarred by the women who abused him."

"Your husband is right, Mrs. Powell."

Felicity sighed. "I can try to be less direct with him. I'm not used to watching what and how I say something, but I guess that comes with the territory of helping an inmate."

"That's a good attitude to have, Mrs. Powell. I will work with Jeff on his issues and move him down a path of forgiveness."

"Thank you, Mrs. Sawyer. I appreciate your help with this."

Mrs. Sawyer packed up her materials and Rick helped her carry them back to her car.

When he got to the top step of the porch, he told Felicity, "I don't want to leave you alone with Jeff until we know more."

"That's not necessary, Rick. I can take care of myself."

"It's not you I'm worried about getting hurt."

Rick caught Felicity's lips turning upward for a split second.

"If I will be away for long-periods of time, I'll take Jeff with me. I'd feel okay if I were close by in the stables or pens just in case something happens."

The next two weeks were like it was before the pizza incident. Felicity was careful about how she spoke to Jeff, and it seemed to help.

At least that's what Rick thought.

CHAPTER FIFTEEN

Rick pecked on the laptop keyboard while sipping sweet tea on the porch when Sergio came up the steps.

"The track to the big door for the stable broke off yesterday. My guys can't stay late, but I'd like to get it on tonight, so I could use your help."

Rick dropped his feet off the wicker ottoman. "Let me fire off this email, and I'll be right down."

Rick and Sergio gathered at the front of Sergio's truck. They drew up plans to fix the door in the dust on his hood like kids drawing up a football play in the playground.

Inside, Felicity was in the kitchen preparing dinner when Jeff strolled into the kitchen and leaned against the counter. He shoved pretzels in his mouth until the bag was empty.

After Felicity dodged Jeff's lanky body planted in the kitchen for the third time, she said, "Dinner's not ready yet. If you want to hang out in your room, I'll give you a yell when it's ready."

"You don't have to treat me like a little kid."

Felicity stopped and smiled, "I'm sorry, Jeff, I'm not trying to treat you like a child. I'm just running around and trying to get everything ready. It's best if nobody is in my way."

"Just because I have these chips under my skin, you think you can control me," Jeff hissed with his jaw clenched.

Felicity took a step back and turned to the counter where her cell phone was charging. Jeff noticed and put his hands up to surrender. "Ah, trying to show me who's boss again. I get it. You're the boss. I'll do as I'm told and go to my room."

Jeff strutted back to his room. After the door closed, Felicity exhaled and ran her fingers through her hair. She stared at the closed bedroom door, expecting it to burst open like the screen door did.

The overflowing pot of boiling pasta was a hasty reminder that dinner also wanted her attention. Felicity released her gaze from the guest suite door and resumed cooking.

She drained the water and put the pot full of pasta back on the cooling burner. A creaking noise came from behind her. It sounded like it came from the end of the dark hallway. She turned and saw the light shining under the closed bedroom door.

"Rocky, is that you?" Her voiced cracked.

Rocky didn't appear by her side like usual when called. Felicity tossed the washed romaine lettuce over the strainer in the sink. She looked out the window. Rick was putting supplies in the back of Sergio's truck. Rocky was right next to Rick.

She took a step back from the sink and peered down the hallway. The door was open.

Felicity spun and snared a towel. In an instant, she wiped both hands, threw the towel and turned toward the front door. As soon as the towel hit the counter, Felicity sensed her feet leave the floor. She slammed against the wall with enough force to knock the wind out of her.

Felicity struggled to get her breath and turn her head to see the perpetrator. Her mouth was covered with one hand while the other held both of her hands behind her lower back. Felicity could smell body odor and cheap aftershave. It was Jeff.

"How do you like it? It doesn't feel so good when you can't move," Jeff whispered into Felicity's ear in a raspy voice.

Felicity tried to turn her head to yell, but Jeff clenched his hand over her mouth with more force each time. He leaned into her and applied his full weight. "Who's in control now?"

Felicity felt the rivets in Jeff's jeans push into her back. Jeff was wearing socks, and he slipped on the hardwood floor each time he adjusted his position for better leverage. That meant his feet were vulnerable.

Felicity waited for the right opportunity to make her move. She had to hit just the right spot. He slipped again, bumping her foot with his toes and Felicity stomped her boot heel onto the center of his foot with all the power she could generate. Jeff yelped in pain and released his grip.

Felicity broke for the front door. She slipped on the hand towel on the floor, but quickly regained her footing and passed under the archway leading to the family room. She could see Rick and Sergio through the glass on the front door. They were oblivious to the battle to save her life taking place a hundred feet away. She tried to scream, but Jeff grabbed her arm just above the elbow before she could find her voice. "Why you little…"

He pulled Felicity back into the kitchen and chucked Felicity across the kitchen toward the table.

Jeff may try to kill me. I have to stop him or attract the guys' attention.

Mid-spin, Felicity swiped a glass off the counter. The glass shattered on the hardwood floor. It wasn't loud enough to activate Sure Cuffs.

Felicity flopped on the kitchen table and flipped to the other side. The high velocity of her drop drove her head into the floor. She tried to get up, but the pain in her ribs and head was blinding. She could hear Jeff stomping toward her but could barely move, let alone shout "wookie." Was this the end?

Felicity opened her eyes and black overtook her vision. She collapsed near the kitchen table.

· · ·

Rick leaned into the bed of Sergio's truck to pull out a toolbelt when Rocky began barking. It was a different tone. An urgent bark. He was moving in circles whining and barking at the end of the sidewalk. Rick took several steps toward Rocky and he darted to the front door. Something was wrong. Rick felt the hair on his neck rise and he broke into a full sprint toward the front door.

Rick pulled so hard on the screen door that it slammed back shut. He yanked it open again and dashed through the door in a single motion. He stopped inside for a second and heard activity in the kitchen.

Rick dashed toward the sound. Between strides, he saw Jeff moving toward a heap of clothes and hair. Rick recognized it was Felicity. The final seven steps were the longest of his life.

Rick yelled "wookie" and dove. Jeff's legs snapped together and his arms pinned to his sides. Rick tackled Jeff onto the kitchen table like a middle linebacker. They rolled off together next to Felicity. Rick saw that Felicity's eyes were open, but her hazy stare told him she wasn't fully aware of the situation. The cut on her forehead was bleeding. A light stream of blood flowed into her hair.

Rick rolled Jeff over, grabbed him by the collar, and demanded "Why? How could you do this? She did nothing to you."

Jeff winced and groaned, but said nothing.

Rick let go of Jeff and scooted over to Felicity. He kneeled beside her, his mouth inches from her ear. "Honey, are you okay?"

She looked at the wall and then the ceiling. "I don't know," she croaked.

"Can I help you up?"

"I… I think so."

Rick put one arm around Felicity and helped her to a sitting position. Felicity blinked every other second. Her usual warm tone left her face. She fixed her gaze on Jeff lying on the floor and didn't look away.

"Honey, don't worry about him. I'll help you into a chair."

Rick called 911.

Jeff yelled out, "you're not going to just leave me here like this, are you?"

Rick strode over to him, wanting to give him a kick in the gut, but Felicity shook her head slightly, so he just gave him a fierce look. "Stay put, and not another word!" he said in a tight voice.

Several minutes later, a sheriff's deputy pulled into FireSky Ranch. Rick met him on the front sidewalk.

"My wife was attacked. The inmate is on the kitchen floor, and he's secure."

More members of law enforcement arrived after the sheriff, including some from TDCJ. One officer tended to Felicity's wounds while the others put traditional cuffs on Jeff and transported him to the back of the deputy's car.

"Mr. Powell, I'm Officer Bryan Hartley from the Office of the Inspector General. I need to ask you a few questions."

An ambulance siren wailed in the distance.

"You'll have to ask at the hospital because I need to go with my wife right now."

The paramedics placed Felicity on a stretcher and fixed an oxygen tube under her nose. Two uniformed men loaded her through the open door of the ambulance. Once they secured Felicity, Rick found his seat in the back beside her. He pushed her hair back from her cut on the way to the emergency room with one hand and held her hand with the other. Rick remembered the last time he was in the back of an ambulance leaving FireSky Ranch. It changed his life forever. Rick closed his eyes and said a quick prayer for his wife.

Once they stabilized Felicity in the Emergency Room, Rick pulled a chair next to her bed. A full rerun of *Seinfeld* finished while a nurse and then a doctor examined Felicity. She needed six stitches to close the wound just above her right eye. While the two women in white coats bent over Felicity, Rick's thoughts drifted to home. The image of Jeff standing over Felicity burned hot on his brain like a cattle brand. His heart beat faster as he recounted his steps trying to determine how he could have arrived sooner.

The white-coated women removed their gloves and disappeared behind the curtain. Rick and Felicity turned their attention back to the movie starting on TV. The color in Felicity's face returned, but she was silent. Rick didn't like the look of the large bump on her head.

Minutes after the credits for *The King's Speech* ended, the ER doctor pushed aside the curtain. "Mrs. Powell, you have a concussion. Everything else looks normal, but you'll need to stay overnight for observation."

Rick leaned back and exhaled.

CHAPTER SIXTEEN

After Felicity fell asleep, Rick left to find a vending machine. He was getting light-headed after missing dinner. Officer Bryan Hartley from the Office of the Inspector General was in the waiting room.

"Mr. Powell, I know you've had a long day, but I need to get your statement."

Rick sat in the chair next to Officer Hartley. "Okay, let's make this quick."

Rick gave his statement to the officer. After a short period of silence, Rick slapped both hands on the armrest, saying, "I'm starving."

"Mr. Powell, did you hear what happened to inmate Stratton?"

"What do you mean? I assume he's back in prison where he belongs."

"He suffered a broken collarbone, and a separated shoulder during your altercation."

Rick stood up and said, "I wouldn't call that an altercation. I was preventing him from attacking my wife any further."

"Sit down, Mr. Powell; we're not done here."

Rick glared at the officer. Speechless, he sat back down.

"I'm curious, Mr. Powell, about why you had to tackle Mr. Stratton after you said the emergency word. Did it not work?"

"Yes, it worked."

"So why did you tackle him if Sure Cuffs immobilized him?"

"I told you, he was attacking my wife!"

"Hmm," Officer Hartley said he scribbled a few lines in his legal pad. "Okay."

This time Officer Hartley stood up. "Mr. Powell, I've heard about you and how you treat your staff. I know you like to get physical with anyone who crosses you."

"What?" Rick threw up his hands and shook his head.

"Blake Highsmith ring a bell?"

"What's Blake have to do with my wife getting attacked by one of your inmates?"

"He's my brother-in-law, Mr. Powell, and we're on the same softball team. He told us all about how you got rough with him when you didn't like what he was doing and fired him on the spot."

Rick rose and moved closer to Officer Hartley, "I didn't lay a hand on him. But I did tell him several times the safe way to lunge a horse, and he kept ignoring me. That's insubordination. I can't work with someone who refuses to follow directions and endangers the animals."

"I think I know what Blake was talking about now."

Rick clenched his jaw and glared at the officer but didn't say another word.

Officer Hartley slipped his pen into his shirt pocket. "I'd be careful if I were you. You don't want to cross that line. Assaulting an inmate is still assault. You don't want to be joining Mr. Stratton in your own cell on D block someday."

Rick shook his head. The nerve of this cop, threatening him.

Officer Hartley gave a forced half smile and said, "Have a good evening, Mr. Powell. Oh, and I hope Mrs. Powell has a speedy recovery."

Rick sat back down in the chair and stared at the eggshell-white wall after Officer Hartley left. He couldn't believe what had just happened.

After breakfast, Rick met Sergio and Alex, one of the FireSky crew, in the parking lot when they dropped off Big Red. A couple hours later, Rick signed the discharge papers and drove Felicity home. He pulled up in front of the house and walked around to the passenger door. When he opened it, Felicity inched out of the truck, but she froze at the sight of the farmhouse.

"Are you okay?" Rick asked as he put his arm around her waist to help her up the sidewalk.

"It's different this time. I'm sure I'll be fine, but this is harder than I thought."

"Do you want to sit outside for a few minutes first?"

"No, let's go inside."

Once inside, Felicity ambled around the kitchen. She examined the counter and kitchen table like a crime scene detective processing each new piece of evidence. Rocky stuck by Felicity's side like glue.

"I'm tired. I need to sit down for a few minutes."

Rick jumped up and hurried over to Felicity's side. He grabbed her arm in the same place Jeff did the day before.

"Ouch, that hurts!" she yelped.

"Oops. sorry." Rick immediately switched the position of his hands and helped Felicity over to her favorite chair in the family room.

"Here's the remote. I bet there's a nice Hallmark movie on somewhere." Rick took a few steps back. "Will you be okay if I check on Sergio and the guys for a few minutes?"

"Yes. I'm just going to hang out here for the rest of the day."

"Great, call me if you need something. I'll be back in two hours."

Ricked called Rocky, "Come on, boy. You coming with me?"

Rocky crouched at Felicity's feet and didn't budge.

"Take care of her, Rocky. I should have listened to you the day the TDCJ dropped him off."

As Rick was coming back from the south end, his phone beeped as soon as he got a signal on his phone. He saw three missed calls from McKenna and a voicemail from Cody.

So far, he'd only had time to text them with a quick update in the ambulance and called them with a few details while in the ER. It was time to give them the full explanation.

Rick pulled over and found McKenna's number. He took a deep breath and dialed. Rick prepared for an argument.

McKenna answered, not with "Hello" but with "How is she?"

Rick explained the entire situation. "She's resting now," he concluded.

"Thank God she's okay."

"Keep praying for her. She's still pretty shaken up."

"I will, Dad. I'm coming home for the weekend, so I'll see you on Friday night."

They hung up with no mention of RIHARP or Jeff.

The call with Cody was similar. He asked where "the prisoner" was, but that was it. He was far more concerned about his mother. Rick hung up and looked over the steering wheel at the vast field of hay. After a quick nod and a deep smile, he threw Big Red into drive and continued back to the farmhouse.

Three days later, Felicity was acting like her old self again. Rick walked up behind her as she was trimming fresh-cut flowers over the sink. He kissed her on the neck, just below the ear.

"How is your head?"

"Much better. The flowers are beautiful."

"Good."

Rick leaned against the counter and crossed his arms. "Honey, I'm sorry about what happened. I never should have let someone in this house who could hurt you. I am going to—"

Felicity cut him off. "You don't need to apologize. I made a mistake letting my guard down and it won't happen again."

"It wasn't your fault at all."

"When will Jeff be coming back to the ranch?"

"Coming back? He's never coming back! He'll spend the rest of his sentence behind bars."

"I never thought turning around the life of a prison inmate would be easy. We can't just quit at the first problem," Felicity said, her eyes tearing up.

Rick slid over to Felicity and cupped his hands under her chin. "Honey, that's not an option. Jeff is no longer eligible for RIHARP because of the attack. He'll likely get more time added to his sentence and have to serve out his remaining years inside the prison walls."

"Can we request a new inmate? I was serious about wanting to help someone."

Rick turned and looked out the window over the sink—the same one Felicity looked out the night she was attacked.

"I don't think that's a good idea. We tried, and it didn't work out. Plus, our kids have been livid with us since the day Jeff arrived. I want to try something else instead."

"I thought we needed the money."

Felicity didn't know how right she was. He opened his mouth and closed it.

"What?"

Now wasn't the right time, so he said, "Sure, any extra money is nice to have, but we don't *need* that money from RIHARP. I have other options to make up the difference. I've got it under control."

Felicity examined Rick's face. A poker player trying to determine a bluff.

"That's good to hear, but I'd still like to consider another inmate in the future."

"I'll keep an open mind, but I need a break from the Texas Department of Criminal Justice."

Felicity laughed. "I can see your point on that."

CHAPTER SEVENTEEN

Rick drove Big Red from the south end to meet a potential new client, a high school friend of Cassie. He hoped he could convince her that FireSky Ranch is the right home for her quarter horse, Pongo.

The meeting went well, and she agreed to lease a stall for six months. It was Rick's first new lease in three months, and he was giddy with the news.

"Sergio, please have someone clean up stall eight. We're going to have a new tenant." Rick said with a wide smile.

"Really? That's great news, Mr. Powell."

"Sure is, Sergio. I could use a few more like this, but I'll take this one today."

When Rick told her the good news, Felicity suggested going into town for lunch and to tackle some additional items on her to-do list. As they began to pull away in Big Red, Rick yelled out to Sergio, "Be sure to secure everything outside the stables. The weather is calling for some strong storms later today."

Several hours later, they were on their way back to FireSky

Ranch. Rick leaned over his steering wheel to get a better view of oil-black cumulus clouds growing in the west. He hit the gas.

"Heading to a fire?" Felicity asked as she was pushed deeper into the plush seats of Big Red.

"I don't like the look of this storm. I want to be sure we batten down the hatches before it hits."

"Just don't get us killed trying to beat it."

Rick leapt out of the truck the instant he cut the engine. The wind was whipping up dust in the pens and he saw workers pulling nervous horses into the stables.

Sergio yelled "Mr. Powell, can you grab the mare in the round pen? We're running out of time before the storm hits."

Rick ran to the round pen as the sky darkened. The chestnut mare was running around the pen, ears back and eyes rotating in all directions on high alert. After each clap of thunder or slamming door, she flinched and tensed up. Rick took a deep breath and slowed his pace. He couldn't rile her up any more. After a minute of inching toward her, sweet talking, Rick was able to grab her lead and said, "Let's go, girl. It looks like it might hail soon."

As Rick left the round pen, he looked to the open pasture in the southwest and froze. The hair on his arms stood up. Before him loomed the largest funnel cloud he'd ever seen in all his years in Texas. It was on the ground and it was tossing debris in all directions—and heading straight for FireSky Ranch.

Rick estimated he only had a couple of minutes before it hit. The mare tossed her head anxiously, and Rick fought to keep her under control as he led her to the stable at a jog. He secured her stall lightning-fast and ran through the building calling a warning: "Tornado! Get to the storm shelter! Tornado! Run!"

Rick saw Sergio gather five other people and start running toward the house where storm doors led to a shelter in the basement.

"Okay, six of them. Looks like Sergio has everyone," Rick muttered to himself.

Tornados are part of life in this part of Texas, so everyone knew what to do. But despite the regular appearance of tornados, each one felt like an ominous threat to life and property.

Rick sprinted back to the house. He ran through the front door and yelled, "Felicity, get to the basement. A tornado is coming!"

He didn't see or hear Felicity. Rick yelled again, louder so his voice could carry above the winds howling outside.

Rick ran upstairs. Felicity was not in the bedroom or bathroom. She wasn't in the office or the kids' bedrooms. He heard enormous rain drops pelting the windows as he descended the stairs. He checked the kitchen and her sewing room.

Where could she be? Her car was still here, and so was her horse. Should he call her cell phone?

He reached into his pocket and heard someone yelling. Rick moved quickly to the window and saw Felicity in the yard shouting for others.

"Oh, no!"

Rick jumped off the front porch and ran toward Felicity yelling in the rain. "Rick? Rick?" Her blond hair was whipping back and forth across her face.

"Felicity, I'm here. Let's head to the shelter. Everyone else is down there." He grabbed Felicity's hand and hurried to the shelter's double doors. He pulled one side open and held it against the force of the wind trying to slam it shut. "Get in."

Felicity started down the stairs and Rick turned around to get one last glimpse of the twister. It was entering the south edge of FireSky Ranch and looked like it was a mile high and as wide as his barn. He could see posts and pieces of fence shooting in all directions from the bottom of the funnel like a bowling ball bursting through pins. He sent up a prayer for the horses locked in their stalls. They were sitting ducks.

"Rick, let's go," Felicity yelled from the bottom of the stairs.

Hail bombarded Rick. He covered his head with one hand and turned to jump through the door, but the wind slammed it shut as soon as he released his grip.

Rick yanked on the door against the gale force winds and hail.

He looked over his shoulder and saw the debris twisting near the south stable. It was less than two hundred yards away. He pulled with all his might and it opened far enough for him to dive into the shelter. The door slammed behind him.

He hurried down the stairs to meet Felicity near the door of the basement. Hail pummeled the door faster and louder. They shut the basement door behind them and saw the dim outlines of Sergio and the rest of the staff sitting silently against the concrete walls. Rick and Felicity huddled together on a wooden bench in the corner.

The twister must have rotated closer to the farmhouse, because the sounds from outside grew louder still. Doors slammed and debris from FireSky Ranch and nearby properties battered the house. It felt like a train was rolling overhead and the basement was under the tracks. Everyone jumped when they heard glass break above them in the kitchen.

A minute later, the deafening noises outside began to diminish. Soon, the only sound was the constant purr of rain.

Rick stood up. "Is everyone okay?"

Sergio looked around to his crew, who all nodded. "Yes, Mr. Powell. Scared, but okay."

Rick looked at Felicity. "How about you?"

"The same."

Rick looked at the stairs leading up to the kitchen. "I'm a little afraid of what I'm going to find when I go up there."

Nobody said a word as Rick crept up the stairs.

He opened the door to the kitchen and was pleasantly surprised. Everything appeared to be intact. He walked into the family room and saw leaves and branches on the floor. That was the window they heard break.

The rain outside slowed to a light sprinkle as Rick walked off the porch. He noticed one of the large oaks in the yard was torn in half and dozens of roof shingles had blown into the yard.

He turned to the stables, groaned "Oh, no!" and wobbled at the sight.

"Sergio, Sergio, come quick!" Rick yelled before he dashed toward the stables. The west side of the south stable was missing.

Sergio emerged from the basement with the rest of the staff and ran in the same direction as Rick.

When Rick got to the damaged stable, he could view the interior through the new, unplanned opening. Only four of the sixteen stalls had horses and they were clearly spooked by the traumatic event. Rick paused to assess the situation. It would have been a different result had the roof of the north stable collapsed or even the east side of the new stable. Horses would have surely been injured or killed. None of that happened.

Rick looked up through the opening.

Thank you, God, for answering my prayer!

Sergio's team tended to the horses and tried to calm them down. Ten minutes later, they transferred the two horses on the west side over to the east side of the stable underneath its intact roof.

"Everything else seems to be okay, Mr. Powell," Sergio said as he walked inside the damaged stable.

"I'm glad everyone and the horses are all okay. It looks like the worst of it missed the house and stables by ten or twenty yards. Thank God!"

Looking up at the rain running off the roof into the stable, Sergio said, "Looks like this roof will need some work, Mr. Powell."

Rick shook his head. "The whole thing might have to be redone. It won't be cheap. For now, let's get the team, clean up as much as we can, and call it a day. I'll get to work on how we are going to repair this tomorrow."

CHAPTER EIGHTEEN

The insurance claims adjuster walked the grounds of FireSky the next day. He took notes on his clipboard and snapped pictures with his phone as he walked around the farmhouse and through the south stable.

Rick watched him from the kitchen window. After gathering information, the adjuster sat in his silver sedan for thirty minutes. Rick could see that he was talking to someone on the phone.

The adjuster exited his vehicle and set his sights on the farmhouse.

Rick met him on the porch just outside the front door, barefoot and in a t-shirt, his hands stuffed in his jean pockets "Did you get everything you need?"

"Yes, Mr. Powell, thank you."

"Great, when will I get the check for the repairs?"

The adjuster cleared his throat and shifted his weight.

"I'll leave you with a check, but it won't cover all the repairs. Not for the stable."

Rick pulled his hands out of his pockets and threw them into the air. "Why not?"

The adjuster turned the clipboard and handed it to Rick. "The damaged stable wasn't on your policy."

Rick yanked the clipboard out of his hand. The adjuster moved next to Rick and pointed at the policy. "None of the improvements you've made in the past two years have been added to the policy. Unfortunately, that includes your damaged stable."

Rick stared at the policy, like the intensity of his gaze could magically add the necessary language to cover his stable. A hazy scene of Cassie reminding him to update his insurance policy a couple years ago creeped into Rick's memory. He shook his head and handed the clipboard back to the adjuster.

"I was so busy when I finished the improvements that I forgot. So what does this mean?"

The adjuster smiled as if he was delivering good news. "It means I'll write you a check now to cover the damage to your house and the north stable."

"But, not the more badly damaged stable?"

"I'm sorry, but the check will only cover damage to structures insured under the policy."

Rick wanted to lash out at the adjuster for the pain he was causing, but Rick knew it was self-inflicted. He pushed his anger down and took the check.

Rick called Sergio as the insurance adjuster drove away from FireSky. He asked him to contact some local contractors to get a quote.

The next morning, two contractors came out to give Rick a quote on repairing the stable. Both quotes were higher than Rick was hoping.

"Is there any wiggle room in that?" Rick asked the last contractor after hearing the quote to repair the stable. "I don't need a Cadillac. A Chevy will do for a stable."

"Not a Cadillac. Just two walls and new roof to cover sixteen stalls. I'm not getting rich building and repairing structures for ranchers."

Rick bristled at the terse reply but knew the quote from the contractor wasn't the real problem.

"Fair enough. Let me talk to the bank and I'll let you know when I can get started."

Rick calculated how much money he would need to cover the stable repairs plus some additional operating costs. He told Felicity he was running to Lone Star Bank to deposit the insurance check. He failed to mention that he would also be taking out another loan.

As Rick opened the door to Big Red, he stopped. "I didn't even think to see what the storm did to you." He walked around, inspecting his truck closely, and stopping occasionally to smudge out any blemishes with his thumb. Once he arrived back at the driver side door, he lovingly patted it. "Just a few scratches, Big Red. Nothing that you can't handle."

Rick pulled into Lone Start Bank and backed Big Red into a spot far from any cars that could inflict door dings. He stared at the front entrance for a few seconds and took a deep breath.

"Here goes nothing."

Rick waited a long time to see his account manager, Ryan. He watched other people coming in with file folders and papers that Rick suspected were repair quotes like his. The tornado ripped apart dozens of structures and ranch equipment before it ended its reign of terror outside of Austin. Fortunately, nobody was hurt or killed.

Once Ryan called him in, Rick took a seat and made his pitch for a loan. He'd done this before, but today was different. Ryan was quieter and talked much slower. Rick wondered if Ryan was distracted by something—perhaps it was the flood of new loan requests after the storm.

As Ryan was reviewing Rick's request, a young lady peeked into the office and asked if she could speak with Ryan. They went to her office on the other side of the lobby. Rick turned around and watched them talking and gesturing to him.

"They better not deny my loan," Rick murmured.

Rick stood up when Ryan returned into his office.

"You're not denying my loan are you, Ryan?"

"Please sit down, Mr. Powell. I have some bad news to share with you."

Rick swallowed hard and took a seat. He kept his eyes locked on Ryan's facial expression, looking for any clues for the pending news.

"What is it? Just give it to me straight."

Ryan took a deep breath and said, "We have to take your truck."

"What?"

"You haven't made a payment in over seven months and our auto loan division has issued an order to repossess your truck."

"I thought we rolled that into my last home equity loan. That's why I haven't been sending checks for the bills you've been mailing me."

"Mr. Powell, we discussed all the terms of your last loan right here at my desk. I explained that you couldn't roll an auto loan into it."

Rick grew light-headed. His stomach felt like he was on a roller coaster, plummeting down a hundred-foot drop. "I can't believe this. First my stable blows down and when I come here for help, I'm told I'm going to lose Big Red, too."

"I'm sorry, Mr. Powell. This isn't what we want either."

Rick faced Ryan but didn't see him. He envisioned Big Red being towed away.

"I'll need your keys. Can someone come pick you up?"

Rick bent forward and cradled his face in his cupped hands. After a loud sigh, he stood up abruptly. He pulled his keychain out of his pocket, removed the key to Big Red, and flung it onto Ryan's desk like a poker chip.

"Take care of Big Red."

Ryan grabbed the key and looked up at Rick. "Again, I'm sorry it has to be this way. What do you want us to do with any personal effects we find in the truck?"

"Burn 'em," Rick said and stalked out of Ryan's office.

Rick walked into the parking lot to get one last look at Big

Red. A minute later, a man in his mid-twenties came out of Lone Star Bank and hopped into Rick's truck. He revved the engine, threw it into drive and pulled out of the parking spot.

Rick ran in front of Big Red and held up his hand. "Stop!"

The young man slammed on the brakes, his eyes and mouth wide open.

Rick went to the driver-side door and motioned to roll down the window. The young man sat frozen a moment, eyeing Rick, probably trying to decide if opening the window was a good idea. He chose to roll it down a few inches.

"Can you give me that baseball glove on the seat? It's thirty years old and means a lot to me."

The young man grabbed the glove, rolled the window down enough to fit the glove and passed it to Rick. As soon as Rick backed away from the door, Big Red lurched out of the lot and was gone.

Rick stared at his phone, dreading the call he needed to make. He considered calling Sergio or texting McKenna with a bribe of a home cooked meal, but Rick knew he had to call Felicity and ask her to come pick him up.

He made the call, sat down on the curb with his glove and waited for Felicity. He stared at the empty parking space vacated by Big Red, utterly numb.

Thirty-five minutes later, Felicity pulled into the blacktop lot behind Lone Star Bank. She noticed Rick sitting on the curb with his glove and eased into the spot beside him. He sat motionless for a few seconds and then crawled into the passenger seat of Felicity's SUV.

"What's going on, Rick? Where's your truck?"

Rick slumped his shoulders and looked down. "Big Red is gone. They took 'im."

"Why?"

Rick reached for the radio. "I don't want to talk about it."

Felicity blocked his hand. "I also didn't want to drop what I was doing to drive half an hour to pick you up. What's going on?"

"I'll tell you all about it when we get home. Not now." He turned to his wife.

Felicity flinched, likely noticing his red-rimmed eyes. "That's fine. But I deserve to know what's going on, so we need to talk before you get started on anything else at the ranch."

Neither one spoke another word during the slow march back to FireSky Ranch.

CHAPTER NINETEEN

Rick walked ahead of Felicity into the house. He went straight to the refrigerator and rooted around for something to drink. He settled on a soda. Felicity hung her purse around the back of a chair at the kitchen table and sat down in it. The kitchen table in the farmhouse has hosted many serious discussions and deep belly laughs. It didn't feel the same now. The image of Jeff standing over Felicity on the floor beside the table crept into Rick's consciousness at the sight of its aging wood, and with it, his fear of losing Felicity. It wasn't just the vision in his mind, though, that was stirring up that dread. It was Rick's secrecy about everything financial. He knew he needed to come clean with Felicity, but his desire to avoid disappointing her was a greater driving force.

"The bank repossessed Big Red because I hadn't made a payment in months."

Felicity tilted her head. "Why? How, um...how come you didn't make any payments?"

"I thought I refinanced it six or seven months ago when I got another loan, so I assumed the bills in the mail were a mistake. I found out today it wasn't rolled into another loan, so the bank took Big Red. I could have sworn Ryan told me—"

"How bad is it?" Felicity interrupted.

"What do you mean?"

"The stress, moving loans all over the place, and now the truck you love is taken from you. Something's going on. What is it?"

Rick opened his mouth to talk, but there was no sound. After his second attempt, he said, "I told you, it's tough right now. I took on some loans to build out the second stable and leases are coming in slower than I expected, but it's a temporary blip in business. It'll turn around soon."

"I'm all for a positive attitude, but we also have to be realistic. It's not going in the right direction." An angry flush was expanding across Felicity's face.

"I've got this. You don't need to worry about it."

"You keep saying that, Rick, but I am worried about it. I'm concerned that you're keeping me in the dark about all the finances related to the ranch. I feel like it's worse than you're telling me and you're not willing to admit it."

Rick did not respond. He leaned back in his chair and crossed his arms.

It was silent for almost a minute. Felicity leaned forward and put her elbows on the table. Fixing her stare into Rick's eyes, she said, "We need to sign up for another RIHARP inmate."

Rick leaped from his chair. "What? No way! Not gonna happen!"

"Why not? We need a reliable income more than ever!"

"Because you were attacked! I can't bring another convicted felon into our home. We have to find another way."

"What other way? We need something soon!" Felicity rose, frowning, with her fists on her hips.

"I don't know yet, but I'll find something better than renting our guest suite to a prisoner. I need to get outside so I can fix that stable. That's a key to keeping the income we have."

Felicity walked over to the counter and leaned against it. "Fine. Go ahead and fix the stable. But for crying out loud, keep me in the loop on the ranch finances. They affect me, too."

Rick was already halfway out the door when he replied, "I will."

But how could he? Felicity had supported him this entire journey. She believed in him. If she knew what a mess he'd made, she'd be gone like so many others in his life.

The next day, Rick found Sergio and his crew inside the damaged stable pulling down some broken boards.

"Hey, Sergio. How's it look?"

"Pretty bad, Mr. Powell, but I have some good news."

Rick chuckled with raised eyebrows. "Good news? I'm not used to that. I better sit down."

"The Grant ranch down the road also had major damage from the tornado. One of his damaged barns was empty, so he said anyone willing to tear the whole thing down can keep all the good wood for free. I think it would be enough to fix this stable. We'd need a few thousand dollars to finish the roof."

"Sergio, you're a genius. I'll call the Grants right now and tell them we'll do it. Tell the rest of the team our plan and let's get on it."

The FireSky crew was on the Grant ranch that afternoon. Sergio and his team were on the barn roof removing the good beams when Rick pulled up in Felicity's white SUV. Sergio stopped working and gaped when Rick, not his wife, got out of the vehicle.

Rick stood at the bottom of Sergio's ladder and yelled, "How's it going?"

"Good. Where's Big Red? In the shop?"

"No. Not in the shop. I have to find something a little more budget friendly." Rick turned away to check out the team's progress. "How long do you think it's going to take to tear this barn down?"

"Ah," Sergio started as he surveyed the barn, "five or six days to take it down and then at least a week to rebuild the stable at FireSky."

"Okay, if you can do it faster that'd be great. I'll take double duty at FireSky this week, so you and your crew can focus on this."

Rick tended the ranch from sunup to sundown while Sergio and his crew tore down the barn on the Grant property. He searched online for a replacement truck and found an old Ford pickup for $1,500. It was in Hays County, so Felicity drove him over to see it. Areas of rust outnumbered the faded fire engine red paint, and it had logged more miles than a mission to the moon. But it was all he could afford, and he needed a farm vehicle immediately to manage all that needed to be done with his crew away. Rusty Red would have to be his new chariot to rule over FireSky Ranch.

After a week at the Grant ranch, Sergio and his crew were back at FireSky, much to Rick's relief. They got busy trying to salvage what they could in the damaged stable while repairing it with their recycled materials.

After morning feed and stall cleaning, Rick sat at the old desk in his office on the second floor and looked at the stack of unopened mail, including envelopes with the big red *Past Due* stamps. He couldn't pretend they were invisible any longer. The sting of losing Big Red was still fresh. Rick rifled through mail in the stack.

Several envelopes were notices from his feed supplier.

"Leave me alone. You gave me an extension!" Rick shouted at a notice.

He read months of past due notices from the veterinarian and for Big Red's auto loan. Rick opened a new catalog-size envelope that Felicity signed to accept. Dread filled his stomach as he read the first sentence. FireSky Ranch was in danger of foreclosure.

Rick dropped his head in defeat. He faced his desk for a

minute and then popped his head back up. Desperation overcame Rick. It felt like he was drowning and needed to come up for air.

Could Cassie kick in a little money? Would it be enough? Should he ask Jack? He said he had savings and offered to help. Could he live with asking Little Jack for money?

They'd probably give Rick the money if he requested it, but that was really the crux of the problem. Rick's eternal status as the family baby was solidified during his lingering grief after his father passed away. Cassie and Jack were back into their daily routine weeks later, but not Rick. His entire life was knocked off balance for years afterward. Everyone tried to help him heal, but they only made Rick feel like he was forever frozen at age fifteen —too immature to be trusted with anything important.

Thirty years ago, Rick sat on the picnic table near Half Moon Creek and vowed he'd make it on his own. Always overshadowed by the ambitions of his older brother or sister, Rick felt he couldn't catch the eye of the older family members who could validate his unique abilities. Rick ran into that brick wall too many times to do it again. He'd never need his family to help him succeed before.

Was it time to admit that a little help wouldn't be the end of the world? Rick pulled his phone from his pocket and scrolled to Cassie's number. He stared at the number as if it were Cassie herself giving him one of her mother-hen pitying looks. He put the phone back in his pocket and went downstairs.

He was prepared to do something once inconceivable.

CHAPTER TWENTY

Rick strolled into the kitchen, where he found Felicity at the table, mending curtains damaged in the tornado. "Hey honey, you got a minute?"

She set down her needle. "Sure, what's up?"

"I've been thinking a little more about what you said about getting another RIHARP inmate. The steady income would be nice to have now."

Rick was expecting a smile or at least a positive reply from Felicity. Instead, she asked, "Why the sudden change of heart? Are finances so bad that you'll open our home to a prisoner again?"

"I thought this is what you wanted!"

"It is, but I know you've been dead set against it. You trust no one, especially anyone with a criminal past, so I'm just wondering why today you're all for RIHARP."

Rick took a step back and put both hands up. "Whoa, where's this coming from?"

Felicity's gaze locked in on Rick like a hunter with prey in his sights.

Rick pointed out the window to Rusty Red. "That's why, okay. I have a stable to fix, a business to build and a crappy car I'm not sure will start when I turn the key. You know we need the money."

Felicity's laugh was menacing as she stood. "I'm not sure how much I *know* of anything, but I can *see* why you've changed your mind."

Rick took a step back away from Felicity.

Felicity moved closer to Rick. "If we do this, we need to do this right. A measly two thousand dollars won't fix our problems. We need to go all in. We need four thousand dollars a month."

"That means a maximum-security prisoner!" Rick bellowed.

"It does."

"I'm not sure I feel comfortable with that."

"No more band-aids, Rick. We need to dig ourselves out of this hole once and for all. I'm not willing to go half-way this time."

Rick paced in the kitchen. He peered out the window and pictured his grandfather building the first stable and his dad training horses in the round pen. Rick knew he was months, maybe weeks, away from losing generations of Powell legacy. Felicity was right. Going all-in with RIHARP really was their best option to bring in much-needed cash fast.

Rick put both hands on the counter near the sink. He leaned over to see Rusty Red in the space where Big Red used to sit. Rusty Red looked as sick as Rick felt.

He sighed, "Okay. Let's do it."

He followed Felicity into the family room. She sat on the couch and opened her laptop. Rick took a seat next to her as they started a new RIHARP application.

Under the question, "What security level are you willing to accept for a RIHARP inmate?" Felicity selected "Maximum Security Inmate."

Her finger hovered above the enter button. She turned to Rick. "Are you sure?"

"Not really, but let's do it. We have a lot to lose either way."

Felicity punched the enter button to submit their application.

· · ·

The same investigators from the Texas Department of Criminal Justice that interviewed Rick and Felicity before Jeff arrived contacted them again. Everything was proceeding without a hitch until Felicity received a call from Officer Bryan Hartley.

"Rick, an officer from OIG is coming to the ranch tomorrow night. He said it's policy for an officer to investigate any re-applications for RIHARP after a failed attempt."

"What's his name?"

"It was a Ryan, or Bryan Hartley I believe."

"Oh great, not that guy again."

"Who is he? I don't remember talking to him during the last application."

"He was the guy that grilled me in the hospital after the incident with Jeff. I got the impression he was trying to pin the blame on me for their psycho inmate. He's a real treat."

Three days later, Officer Hartley pulled into FireSky Ranch and parked behind Rusty Red. He did a complete turn and digested the layout of the ranch. Then he drifted up the sidewalk to the front door as if he was looking for clues in a crime scene.

Rocky noticed him first and growled louder with each step Officer Hartley got closer to their porch.

"Put Rocky in the laundry room," Felicity told Rick.

"I don't know; maybe this guy won't stay long if we keep him out."

"Rick!"

He reluctantly led Rocky to the laundry room and shut the door.

Felicity let Officer Hartley in and invited him into their kitchen. Rick joined them and sat down.

"Thank you for meeting with me today, Mr. and Mrs. Powell. The Texas Departments of Criminal Justice is responsible for all RIHARP inmates, so I'm here to ensure this environment is a good fit."

Officer Hartley sat down and opened his leather-bound notepad.

"I've read the report I took at the hospital, and the statement from Mr. Stratton and I noticed inconsistencies. I want to get clarification on what happened with Mr. Stratton so we can wrap up this case."

Felicity and Rick looked at each other.

"I'll do the best I can. The night is still foggy for me," Felicity shared. She hoped the concussion hadn't blacked out too much of her memory. It seemed important to have the details right.

"Thank you, Mrs. Powell. Most of the inconsistencies occurred with Mr. Powell and his response to Mr. Stratton when he entered the kitchen that evening."

Officer Hartley flipped the page.

"Mr. Powell, according to Mr. Stratton, he was struggling with Mrs. Powell when you entered, saw the struggle and yelled the emergency word to activate Sure Cuffs. As a result, Mrs. Powell lost her balance, hit the table and fell to the floor. When you saw your wife on the floor, you became furious and charged the defenseless inmate and tackled him over the table. He suffered a broken clavicle and a separated shoulder."

Felicity couldn't believe what she was hearing. "That's not what happened. Jeff slammed me against the wall and threw me over the table so hard I got a concussion. He was coming at me again when Rick came in and tackled him."

"Thank you, Mrs. Powell, but I'd really like to hear your husband's side of the story again." Hartley glared at Rick, waiting for a response.

Felicity fumed. Not only did the officer dismiss her story, he made it sound like her husband attacked an innocent old man sitting peacefully on a park bench.

Rick shook his head and glared at the officer. "My wife just told you what happened."

"Are you confirming his account, Mr. Powell?"

"I'm confirming you are taking the word of a convicted criminal over the person he attacked, over a family who opened their home to help him!" Rick seemed to be getting a bit belligerent.

Felicity wondered what had happened between these two at the hospital.

Officer Hartley's lip curled in a sneer. "That's not true, Mr. Powell. That's why I'm here today, to get the correct story so I can determine the fitness of this family to host another RIHARP inmate."

Rick's ears turned red, and his eyes narrowed. "My answer today is the same as when you took it in the hospital. I heard the struggle outside, and when I entered the house, I saw Jeff standing over Felicity lying motionless on the floor. I didn't think of anything, and I ran toward him as fast as I could. When I was a few feet away, I yelled wookie, and Sure Cuffs activated just as I tackled him. No premeditated rage that Jeff has sold to you. Just a husband scared to death for his wife's life trying to stop the attacker. Is that clear enough for you?"

"It tells me a lot, Mr. Powell. I'll complete my report and submit it to the OIG. You'll hear from me if I have additional questions."

Officer Hartley showed himself to the door.

Felicity couldn't keep her eyes off her husband. "What was *that* all about?"

"He's Blake Highsmith's brother-in-law and softball buddy. I hope this doesn't hurt our chances of getting a new inmate."

It didn't. RIHARP awarded Felicity and Rick a new maximum-security inmate.

A man convicted of murder.

CHAPTER TWENTY-ONE

Rick and Felicity admired the deep blue of the cloudless sky as they waited for their new inmate. They turned and watched two familiar GMC Yukon SUVs descend the gravel road to FireSky Ranch once again. After both vehicles pulled in front of the farmhouse, an officer emerged from one and walked around to the rear passenger side door. Felicity and Rick leaned on the porch railing to get a good look at their new inmate. The SUV door opened, and a man in an orange jumpsuit with short, curly, black hair emerged from the back seat.

Rick gasped. He read in the file that the inmate was six-feet-four-inches tall and weighed two hundred and twenty pounds, but Rick thought he looked even bigger.

The inmate had a somber expression as he climbed out of the back seat. Once he took a few steps, he stopped. He looked left, right, and then up at the sun drifting down in the western sky. He smiled wide, and Rick noticed that he was missing his right upper canine tooth.

Two officers were on each side of the inmate as they escorted him up the sidewalk. Rick and Felicity gave each other a quick glance and left the porch to meet their new houseguest. Rocky joined the welcoming party.

The officer on the left spoke first. "This is James Edmunds, and he will be your new RIHARP inmate."

Felicity extended her hand first, and James reciprocated.

"How do you do, ma'am? Pleased to meet you."

"I'm Felicity. Welcome to our ranch."

James looked at Rick and put out his hand. "Nice to meet you, sir. You have a beautiful ranch."

"Thank you. I'm Mr. Powell. Welcome to FireSky Ranch. It's been in my family for over forty years."

"It's a pleasure to be here, Mr. Powell."

As Rick was shaking James's hand, he noticed Rocky sniffing around James. He leaned over to grab Rocky's collar, assuming he'd growl as he did at Jeff. But Rocky continued to calmly investigate James and sniff his hands, legs, and feet.

The officers worked on their transfer protocol. One officer established the GPS boundaries at the ranch property lines, and the other went inside to explain Sure Cuffs to Rick and Felicity. Just like the last RIHARP transfer, they had to activate Sure Cuffs on James to ensure everything worked. Felicity tucked her hair behind her ears. She quickly replaced it when it came loose. Rick adjusted his shirt and rubbed his nose three or four times as they positioned James in the center of the family room. Just like Jeff.

Rick winced as he activated Sure Cuffs. He looked up to James and was surprised to see his relaxed demeanor. Next, it was Felicity's turn. She cleared her throat.

"It's still wookie," Rick reminded her.

"I know."

The emergency word came from deep within Felicity, like the volume needed to match the size of the inmate. Sure Cuffs activated and James had the same demeanor as the first time. Rick and Felicity both exhaled, relieved by James's reaction to Sure Cuffs. Felicity let her hair fall over her ears and didn't re-tuck it.

The officers completed the transfer and packed everything to leave.

"Is Mrs. Sawyer coming this time?" Felicity asked.

"No, ma'am. Mrs. Sawyer couldn't make it this time, but she'll schedule another time for an on-site visit," an officer reported.

Once the TDCJ officers left, Felicity informed James that a new set of clothes was available for him in the guest room. She started down the hallway and abruptly stopped.

"Rick, could you show James to his room? Be sure to show him the drawers with his new clothes and the towels and washcloths for his shower. He should have a few pairs of new jeans, t-shirts and a pair of work boots that fit him."

After Rick gave James the tour and told him to get familiar with the room, he found Felicity alone in the kitchen.

"You okay?"

"Yeah. It hit me when I started down the hallway. It was one of the last things I remember before Jeff attacked me. Funny how those images can pop up."

"Is James making you uncomfortable?"

"No. I feel good about him. He looked me right in the eye when he shook my hand, and that's not something Jeff ever did."

"So far so good for me, too. It surprised me that Rocky never growled at him. Maybe he senses something in James."

"Could be."

"Either way, I will not make the same mistake I made last time. I'm not leaving you alone with James. Ever!"

Rick walked back to the guest suite and saw James sitting on the bed. He was staring at the wall.

"Hey James, it's been a long day for everyone, and you and I will have an even longer day tomorrow. Get cleaned up and let's call it a night."

James looked over at Rick, "Thank you, Mr. Powell."

"The remote control for the TV is on the nightstand."

James looked at the remote control and then back to Rick. He opened his mouth but didn't say anything.

"Do you need something, James?"

James pointed to a bookshelf full of Elizabeth's books, some still stiff and new and others dog-eared and loved. "What about those books? Can I read them?"

Rick looked to the shelves. "Are you a big reader?"

James nodded. "Yeah, ever since I was in the Army. I like the freedom they provide."

Rick tilted his head. "Freedom?"

"Yeah, no matter where I am, when I read, I can disappear to somewhere else I'd rather be. I'd leave Iraq for hours or escape the cold walls of my cell from the beginning of a book to the end. I hated when stories ended because I had to come back to my bunk or cell, but the taste of freedom was delicious when I had it."

Rick was at a loss for words, unsure how to respond to something so deep. He practically whispered, "Read anything you'd like. Good night."

Rick closed the bedroom door and stared at it. "Wow."

Felicity sat in bed with the RIHARP Inmate Profile binder open. She read about where James was born, where he went to high school and his complete personal history. It showed James was sentenced for second-degree murder, but unlike Jeff's file, the Texas Department of Criminal Justice had redacted the details of the conviction.

"Hmm. Not many details on why James was convicted of second-degree murder," Felicity told Rick when he entered the room and began getting ready for bed.

"That sounds so strange to say about a person living in our guest suite below."

Felicity looked up at Rick but did not see him. She tapped her finger on the binder. "Yeah, I guess it does. I'm wondering why they would black out all those details."

"Privacy rules, I'd guess. Do a Google search on his case. I'm sure you can find out more details."

"I intend to."

"What else did you find?" Rick asked as he climbed into bed.

Felicity leaned forward and pulled a pillow out from behind her and placed it on her lap. She leaned over the binder lying flat on the pillow and flipped to the end of the information.

"Overall he seemed to have a relatively normal upbringing with brothers and sisters in the suburbs of Houston. He played football in high school. He was never in trouble before the incident that landed him in prison. He's a veteran."

"He mentioned something about the Army and Iraq."

"It says he served two tours in Iraq. That's everything in his file. It has a lot more holes in it than the file on Jeff."

Felicity pulled the pillow from her lap and put it behind her back again.

Rick's eyes narrowed. "I wonder why."

CHAPTER TWENTY-TWO

The next morning, Rick found James sitting in the dark kitchen, waiting for him.

"You know you can turn on the lights and grab a coffee."

"Okay, Mr. Powell. I didn't want to disturb you or Mrs. Powell.

"I appreciate the gesture, but this is where you will live, so I want you to feel at home here. You know the general rules for the RIHARP program so other than those, help yourself to whatever you need."

James rose slowly from his chair and opened the refrigerator. He pulled out a dozen eggs and looked over his shoulder. Rick nodded with approval.

James opened the lid and smiled. "I haven't had fresh scrambled eggs in a long time. Want some?"

"Sure."

James was nimble in the kitchen for a man of his size and was meticulous with every task. He portioned out the skillet of scrambled eggs onto plates Rick provided and they sat down together to enjoy their breakfast.

Rick watched the man sitting across the table eat his breakfast. He could tell this inmate was different.

"James, this is impressive. How'd you learn to cook like this?"

James put down his fork and looked up. "My grandma. She taught me to do a lot of things."

Next Rick took James to the stables and introduced him to Sergio and his crew. They all fell silent when James and his six-foot-four frame passed through the sliding barn door.

Sergio told his crew leader to take James to the supply room so that he could get comfortable with the supplies.

Sergio asked Rick, "What do you think of this new one? Better than the last guy?"

"Hard to say. I met him for the first time last night, but this guy feels different. Rocky seemed to like him."

"That's a good sign."

"Sergio, I want you to push him. I need to know soon if James will work hard or if he'll break down and buckle under pressure. If we have another Jeff on our hands, I need to know before anything happens to Felicity."

"Sure thing, Mr. Powell. We have plenty for him to do."

The neighbors' negative reaction to a new RIHARP inmate was more intense than the last time. Days after James arrived, Felicity's and Rick's phones blew up with voicemails, texts, and calls voicing their opposition to a new inmate living on FireSky Ranch. Mark Cochran from Circle G ranch called Rick and launched into a two-minute tirade so loud that Rick held the phone away from his ear. Felicity wasn't sure what Mark said, nor did she particularly want to. Clearly, he was not happy with a new criminal in the neighborhood.

Felicity also received her share of complaints. McKenna called first.

"Mom, is it true? I got your message, but I was hoping it was just a bad dream. Do you have a new prisoner living with you?"

"Yes, we do."

"Didn't you learn anything the last time? These criminals are in prison for a reason. You've got to stop inviting them to live with you."

"Your father and I will be much more careful this time. We learned a lot from the last time."

"I'd hope you'll be more careful. I worry you might get attacked again."

The conversation went on like this for another five minutes until Felicity threw McKenna a curveball: "Come stay with us over the Labor Day weekend."

"What?" McKenna gasped. "Will he be there?"

"Yes, James will be here."

"That doesn't sound like a good idea. Or a safe thing to do."

"McKenna Emily, stop being so judgmental of someone you've never met. I feel comfortable around James, and I'd like you to be, too. Have you heard anything Pastor Scott has said about this on Sundays?"

McKenna was silent.

"James will be released back into society in a few years. He will get a second chance to lead a productive life. Just like you and me. He's been in prison for nearly two decades and needs to practice basic social skills. Getting used to interacting with all kinds of people is important for him to succeed. And it's important for you to do the same, sweetheart. Plus, I miss you. I'd really like for you to spend a few nights with us back on FireSky. Please?"

"Will it be safe?" McKenna inquired.

"I promise it'll be safe. I think once you see firsthand all the safety measures that are in place you'll feel better about the whole thing."

McKenna sighed. "Okay, I'll come home. I miss you, too."

The call with Cody was similar. He questioned his mom's sanity and expressed concern for her safety. Felicity applied a Texas-size dose of guilt and Cody also agreed to come home for Labor Day weekend.

Felicity practically danced out to the porch to tell Rick the good news.

"The kids are both coming home for Labor Day weekend!"

Rick set down his *Farm and Ranch Living Magazine* and stared. "Wow, how did you manage that?"

"They were resistant at first, but I applied a strong dose of motherly guilt, and it worked. I think they'll feel a lot better about RIHARP once they're here and can see how everything works."

"I sure hope so. I miss them, and it would be awful if they just stopped coming home."

CHAPTER TWENTY-THREE

Rick met Sergio inside the supply room in the north stable, like they did every morning to start the day. "How's James working out?" he asked.

"He's a hard worker and gets along with everyone, but he doesn't say much."

"He's kind of hard to figure out." Rick slung a few saddles from the bottom shelf up to a top shelf above his head. "I'm hoping he's just a quiet guy and not a volcano waiting to erupt."

"So far so good, I guess," Sergio said.

"Since Labor Day weekend starts tomorrow, let the crew know they should stage enough hay and feed in the stables and water in the pond for a three-day weekend. James and I can handle the daily chores until you get back on Tuesday. The kids are coming down for the long weekend, so I may put them to work, too."

McKenna arrived first. She parked her small, hybrid coupe in front of the farmhouse. Felicity was quick to greet her with a hug before she even made it to the sidewalk. Rick warily joined the welcoming party. Which McKenna was showing up today?

Rick picked up McKenna's bags.

"Staying for a week or two?" Rick asked as she struggled to pull the suitcase out of the small trunk.

"Funny, Dad. I need everything in there."

The tension eased in Rick's shoulders as he took McKenna's bags up to her room while Felicity and McKenna caught up in the kitchen. Minutes later he heard a rumble out front.

"That must be Cody."

Cody arrived in his new lifted extended cab RAM Titan pickup truck. As usual, Cody had his music blaring as he barreled into the parking area.

McKenna, Felicity, and Rick all walked out to greet Cody.

"What do you think, Padre? Nice, isn't it?" Cody gloated as he pulled his gym duffel out from the passenger side of the truck.

"It's great. I'm a little jealous."

"He's my Big Red." Cody glanced around. "Where is Big Red?"

Rick responded, "How was the traffic coming down from Dallas? Seems like you made it down here pretty fast."

Cody walked around Felicity's Ford Explorer and noticed Rusty Red. "Traffic was fine. I want to see if my truck sits higher off the ground than Big Red. Where is he?"

Rick sighed. "We've had to make several changes on the ranch. You'll see a few more of them this weekend."

Cody swallowed hard and broke eye contact. "Is that heap of rust your truck, Dad?"

Rick crossed his arms. The hot tension in his stomach was moving into his chest. He resisted the defensive comments on the tip of his tongue and redirected Cody to his small overnight bag, "I thought you were staying a couple of nights."

"Huh? I am. Why?"

Rick looked over at McKenna with a smile. "No reason."

"Dad, I need everything I brought," McKenna said, laughing as she walked over and punched her father in the arm.

Felicity announced, "Everyone, get settled in your rooms. We're doing lunch on the porch in an hour."

They all found a seat in the shade and enjoyed the Texas barbeque feast prepared by Felicity.

Cody shared a story about his first business trip.

"I was up in Central Illinois with a bunch of other investment specialist trainees and during dinner one of the guys from Boston said we should go cow tipping. I tried to explain it was a myth for city boys like him, but they said they heard previous trainees did it, so he wanted to try. We took two cars outside of town and found a farm with a herd of cows. Six of us jumped the fence and tried to tip a cow, but ended up causing a stampede when two guys got scared and bolted. A guy from Detroit swore he was chased by a bull, but I think they just got scared by some old heifer. The looks on their faces when those cows took off together across the pasture was priceless."

Everyone laughed and then it was McKenna's turn.

"We pulled the best prank on some girls living on our floor. We taped clear saran wrap across their door. Then my roommate knocked real hard to get them to hurry out and see what was going on. They ran right into the saran wrap and freaked out, flopping around and waving their arms like they were getting attacked by an invisible octopus. It was hilarious! We got it all on video."

Once the laughter died down, Felicity said, "It sounds like you are both having fun at your job and school. I hope you are also working hard."

Cody and McKenna exchanged a look, then laughed again and reassured her that they were.

McKenna put her empty plate aside. "How's it going with the new prisoner? Where is he?"

Felicity replied, "his name is James, and he's watering the horses right now. He'll be back in an hour."

"Does he wander around anywhere he wants? I'm not sure I feel comfortable sleeping with him downstairs."

Rick laughed and shook his head. "No, he doesn't just come and go anywhere any time he wants. He's part of the ranch staff with responsibilities, and he has a new technology embedded in him. It limits him to designated areas in the house and on the ranch. He can't go upstairs, or it will activate his Sure Cuffs. If Sure Cuffs are activated, he can't move."

"I guess that explains how you two sleep at night," Cody said.

"What are Sure Cuffs?" McKenna asked. "Are they reliable?"

Felicity explained Sure Cuffs, including all the ways she can activate them.

Cody moved to the edge of his chair. "What's the emergency word? I want to try it on him when he gets back."

Felicity tossed her napkin onto the table. "Cody, he's not a new toy. James is a human being that needs to be in a safe, caring. and supportive environment."

"Fine, but can I try to trick him into going upstairs to see how it works?"

"Of course not, son," Rick said. "We taught you better than that."

When James entered the kitchen, everyone froze. McKenna and Cody edged closer to their mother.

"Cody and McKenna, this is James. He's our new house guest. James, this is our son Cody and our daughter McKenna."

An awkward silence filled the room.

Cody stepped toward James and shook his hand. "Nice to meet you, James."

"You too Mr. Cody."

McKenna moved behind Cody. She bumped into him as they both turned the same direction after Cody's handshake. McKenna let out a nervous laugh.

"Hi James, I'm McKenna."

"Pleased to meet you, Ms. McKenna."

McKenna blushed and giggled at the formality, and Rick and Felicity both laughed.

McKenna and Cody spent Saturday night out with friends. On

Sunday, the Powell family attended church together and then served lunch at the Hill Country Christian Church homeless shelter, a tradition dating back to when Cody was in middle school.

They played several intense games of horseshoes and corn toss. Next, the Powells prepared for one of their favorite family activities – sharing stories around a fire. Everyone found a seat around the fire pit as the shadows took over the yard and the moon became visible above the horizon. Two minutes into Cody's first story, a pickup truck pulled into the parking area.

Rocky charged over to the truck to investigate. A silhouette of a man moved behind his truck. He reached into the bed of his truck and pulled something out.

"I wonder who that is?" Felicity asked.

"Rocky's not barking. That's strange." Rick said.

Everyone stood up and moved toward the vehicle. As they got closer, Rick identified the man.

"Blake? What are you doing here?"

"Where is he?" Blake snarled.

"Where's who?"

"The killer. The murderer that's living with you. That's who!"

"He's inside. What's with the bat?"

"My Louisville Slugger is for protection. I don't like killers roaming free where I live. They belong behind bars, and that's where he should be."

"You've been drinking. Let me call a ride for you."

"Funny how I have more common sense than you even after I've had a few beers. First, you fire me, and then you try to replace me with a cold-blooded killer. What kind of idiot would bring a killer into their home and put all their neighbors' lives in danger?

Rick put both hands in the air and inched closer to Blake.

"Mrs. Powell never would've gotten hurt if you'd kept me on instead of replacing me with that monster," Blake said. "She understands that I could make this ranch what you want it to be but can't. She deserves better."

"Come on, Blake, let's not go there. Let's get you home so you can sleep it off."

"You can still have me, Rick. I'm not working right now. You can send the murderer back to prison and protect your family while I help you straighten out this ranch."

James emerged from the house and stood on the patio.

Blake turned and stomped across the yard like a charging elephant. He stopped at the picnic table near the bottom of the porch stairs.

James didn't flinch.

"You need to be behind bars. You killed someone, and you don't deserve to be free."

James walked down the stairs. He kept his eyes on Blake during each step.

"I'm calling the sheriff to come and pick you up before you kill someone else."

James stopped on the opposite side of the picnic table.

Rick moved swiftly to James's side. "Stay calm, James. He's just trying to bait you."

"Not trying to bait him, but I will defend myself if this murderer tries to attack me. I'll crack my friend Louie here across his head!"

James glided slowly around the picnic table until the six-inch height difference between the two men grew obvious. Blake was within striking distance.

"No!" Felicity screamed.

Blake puffed up his chest and glared at James, "Stay away from me, you murderer. You're going back to prison where you belong."

Blake reared back with both hands over his head and slammed his wooden bat down. The bat made a loud thud as it connected with the picnic table like a lumberjack splitting a log.

Faster than a diamondback rattlesnake strike, James pulled the bat from Blake's hands and smashed it over the decorative boulder near the picnic table.

James pointed the broken half of the bat inches from Blake's face, and in a calm, commanding voice, said, "Go."

Blake took a few steps back, never taking his eyes off James.

"Now!" James roared.

Blake took more steps back and turned back toward his truck. "This isn't over."

CHAPTER TWENTY-FOUR

L abor Day started early for the Powells. Just like old times, Cody and McKenna joined their parents at six o'clock sharp in the north stable. After cleaning the stalls, they all saddled up for a trail ride.

The air was still cool as they cantered through the pasture and trotted along the trail winding around the rolling hills full of Texas live oak trees. Everyone stopped to let the horses drink from Half Moon Creek.

Felicity turned to the kids. "I'm so glad you both came down this weekend. What do you think about everything now?"

McKenna pinched her lips, nodded and replied, "I understand why you are doing this prisoner program. I still have reservations, but I feel better now. I can't believe how calm and cool James was with Blake Highsmith."

"Right? That looked like it was going to get ugly and fast. James showed a lot of patience and self-control."

Cody backed his horse away from the stream. "I have a question. Why did Dad get rid of Big Red?"

Felicity turned to Rick. He cleared his throat and straightened up in his saddle, "Business is flat, Cody. I couldn't afford to keep

Big Red and continue to invest in FireSky." Rick forced a laugh. "I'll replace him with something bigger and better someday."

Cody didn't smile. "Is that all? The ranch seems different. Stuff's broken. I've never seen it like that before."

Rick felt the heat of six eyes on him. Felicity's gaze was especially intense.

"Is this where you pitch your new investment services to me?"

Cody smiled. "It's not like that, Dad. I make sure all the agents are educated on our products and services."

Rick looked at his watch. "We better head back for lunch. Both of you need to pack up before you head off."

After lunch, Cody and McKenna packed their vehicles. Cody left first for his three-hour drive, waving and calling, "I'll be praying for you guys!"

An hour later, Rick and Felicity walked McKenna to her car.

Felicity gave her a hug. "Thanks for coming home this weekend."

"I'm glad I came."

"I can't tell you how happy it makes me to hear you say that. Don't wait too long to come back again for another weekend."

"Okay, Mom, I will."

McKenna gave Rick a stern look. "Take care, Dad."

He knew what she meant: Make sure there's a home to come back to.

The next morning, Rick drove James to the south end to meet Sergio. James would be helping the crew move the pond pump from one location in Half Moon Creek to another spot further downstream.

As they bumped down the pasture access road, James surprised Rick by asking, "Why do you call this FireSky Ranch?"

Rick smiled. "That was my grandpa. At first, it had a very creative and unique name. It was Powell Ranch."

Rick looked over and caught James returning a courtesy grin.

"The real story is my grandpa used to start every day on the ranch before sunrise. Then looking over those east hills, he would watch the sky turn brilliant colors of orange, red, and gold before the sun appeared high in the sky. He said the sky looked like it was on fire just over the ridge, so he changed the name to FireSky Ranch."

Rick turned left down the last patch of road before they reached Sergio in the south end. He put the truck in park but didn't open the door. "My grandpa loved to watch the sun come up. Every time I look at those rolling hills in the east, I think of him. He said he loved to witness the birth of a new day. A brand-new day. A new beginning. Everything from the day before was in the past. We all get a clean slate to live each new day when that sun comes up over those hills."

Rick pointed to the hills to the left through the windshield.

"We're a little late today, but you can still see some fire in the sky.

James bent down to peer under the visor for a better view.

"I like that. Every day is a fresh start," James said in a whisper.

Dinners were quieter with James. He never initiated a conversation.

One evening as the cool breeze rustled the autumn leaves outside the open kitchen window, Felicity put down her fork and asked, "James, we've told you so much about us, but I still don't know a lot about you. I want to learn more about you."

"What do you want to know?"

"Um, tell me about where you grew up, where you went to school."

James shifted in his seat. "I, uh, lived in Houston. That's where I went to school."

"What did your parents do?"

"My dad was an electrician, and my mom was a teacher.

Mom's still teaching but Dad passed away from cancer when I was in the Army."

Felicity leaned forward. "I'm sorry about your dad."

James nodded.

Felicity waited for a response, but after ten seconds of silence she continued with her questions. "What grade does your mom teach?"

"Second."

"What about your brothers and sisters?"

"I have two older sisters and one younger brother."

Rick felt compelled to save James from Felicity's FBI level interrogation. Between questions, Rick asked, "How did you end up in the Army?"

James straightened up in his chair.

"I had a lot of friends over in Iraq after 9/11, so I kept watching the news about the war. I didn't do so good my first year in college, so I decided to join the Army."

"Thank you for your service. Were you in Iraq?"

"Yes, sir. I was stateside my first year in Fort Sill Oklahoma with the 5th Armed Infantry Division, and then I spent two tours in the sandbox over in Iraq."

Nobody spoke for several seconds.

James broke the silence. "It was messed up."

"I'm sorry, James," Felicity replied in a soothing voice. "Is that why you are in prison? Can you tell us what happened?"

James looked down at the table, "I'm sorry, Mrs. Powell, but I don't want to talk about that."

Felicity flashed Rick a look of concern.

CHAPTER TWENTY-FIVE

Felicity put three Cornish hens in the oven and set the timer. They had all been working hard to make the ranch more profitable, so she decided to make a gourmet lunch for everyone as a small reward.

"Oh shoot, I forgot to do something in the supply room," Rick said as he headed to the front door.

"Don't be too long. Lunch will be ready soon."

Felicity watched Rick pass by the round pen and disappear behind the old stable. She snapped peas over the sink.

A creak came from down the hallway.

Felicity jumped and turned toward the guest suite. Light from under the door illuminated the floor planks at the end of the dark hallway. Felicity felt her heart slam into her chest wall. She was breathing like she had just run up a flight of stairs.

Felicity secured her phone.

"James? Is that you?"

Nobody answered from the end of the dark hallway.

Felicity looked at the stove. Eight minutes and eleven seconds left on the timer. She had to finish lunch, but her nerves were getting the better of her.

She placed the phone next to the sink and snapped more peas.

She frequently dropped peas and picked them up again as her hands trembled. The reflection in the window highlighted her ashen face.

More creaks came from the hallway. Somebody was coming toward her. *Please, Lord, not again.*

Felicity grabbed her phone and opened the Sure Cuffs app in a matter of seconds. Her thumb was almost touching the activate button.

"Do you need any help in here?"

Felicity turned to James with her mouth wide open in a silent scream.

"I thought I heard you call for me."

Felicity exhaled and put her phone down. Her legs still felt wobbly as she leaned against the counter. "Yes, I'd love help."

James set the table as Felicity directed. While she worked on the rest of the meal, her heart rate gradually returned to normal. When the timer went off, she removed the Cornish hens from the oven.

Rocky barked at a car out front. A white sedan pulled in, and a young man in his late twenties opened his door a few inches. He clung to his door as Rocky stood with his legs apart and his chest thrown out, baring his teeth.

Felicity called Rocky to the porch and clipped him onto a dog lead. To the man, she called, "What can I do for you?"

"I'm looking for Mr. Richard Powell. I have an important delivery."

Felicity hadn't heard Rick called by that name in years. She left the porch and stopped at the front of the car. "He's in the stable. I'm his wife, I can take it for him."

"I'm sorry, Mrs. Powell, but I can only deliver this to Richard Powell."

Felicity paused for a second and then shook her head.

"Okay, I'll go get him."

. . .

Rick was in the supply room, stacking buckets of supplements for healthy hooves, when Felicity came looking for him.

"There's a man here to see you."

Rick pulled another bucket out of a larger box and placed it on a shelf. "Who is it?"

"I don't know. He said he would only talk to you."

Rick stopped and put his hands on his hips. "Hmm. He didn't say anything else?"

"No, he's waiting for you up front."

Rick took off his work gloves and walked with Felicity.

Neither spoke during the three-minute walk to the parking lot. Rick suspected it was bad news and didn't want to tell Felicity about the ranch's financial situation right now.

Rick approached the young man. "I understand you are looking for me."

"Are you Richard Powell?"

"Yes, I'm Rick Powell."

"Please sign here, Mr. Powell," the man said as he handed Rick a clipboard and a package.

Rick felt it was a small stack of paper. "What is this?"

"I'm not sure, Mr. Powell, but Lone Star Bank wanted to be sure you received these documents. Have a good day."

Rick tore open the package and read the cover letter. It was an official letter with an auction date for FireSky Ranch.

"What is it?" Felicity asked.

Rick rammed the cover letter back into the envelope. "I'm not sure yet. I've got to read all this stuff and I don't have time right now."

Felicity reached for the package. "I can read it for you. I have time."

"No!" Rick snapped.

Felicity pulled her hand away.

"I mean, I want to know what this is about. Give me a couple of hours to finish up out here and I'll be in to read it."

"I don't know why I can't read it. It's from Lone Star Bank, so I assume it's important."

Rick tucked the package under his arm and adjusted his tool belt. "I don't think it's that important, but it's something I'd like to read first. I will let you know what it says. Let me get back to work so I can read this."

"I'm eating lunch without you."

Felicity went inside, and Rick returned to the supply room. He took the package with him. Once inside, Rick read the first couple of pages. It said the bank had set an auction date to foreclose FireSky Ranch in six weeks unless he paid the overdue balance on his account.

He picked up a pipe wrench and then a hammer from the workbench. He bounced both off the wall at the other end of the supply room.

"I can't believe this!" he wailed.

Rick paced back and forth like a newly weaned foal, and then stalked off to find Sergio.

"I need to go visit my mom right now. I'll be back in a few hours."

Rick drove Rusty Red into Austin and parked outside Gentle Breeze Assisted Care Center. He sat in his truck for a few minutes and plotted his next move. His plan required him to do something he swore he'd never do.

Elizabeth Powell was wheeling herself from her room to the community center. A staff nurse followed Elizabeth to her destination. The left half of her lips curled up when she saw Rick.

"What a pleasant surprise."

Rick followed his mom and the nurse to Elizabeth's favorite table. Once she sat down, Rick sat down across from her.

"How are you doing, Mom?"

"Okay. Been fighting a bug."

"Are they taking good care of you?"

"Oh yes, yes. They're great."

"Your speech is getting much better. You must be doing a lot of speech therapy."

"Every single day." Elizabeth let out a quiet cough and motioned to the cards on the table. "Did you come here to play rummy with me?"

Rick looked at Elizabeth and then down at the table. Why not indulge her? He could use the distraction as much as she could. "Yes, I did."

"Great. Nobody around here will play with me anymore."

Rick and his mom played two hands of rummy. It was two more easy wins for Elizabeth, and a blur of suits and numbers for Rick, tangled as his thoughts were in the impending foreclosure.

"You want to play one more?" Elizabeth inquired.

Rick looked at his watch.

"I have time for one more game, but we need to raise the stakes."

"Oh. What is it?"

"Let's play for forty-two thousand, six hundred dollars."

Elizabeth crinkled her nose and lowered her eyebrows. "What do you mean? Play for money?"

Rick looked into Elizabeth's eyes but did not respond.

"I… I'm sorry. I don't understand."

"Yes, I need money. I need forty-two thousand, six hundred dollars in a few weeks or the bank will take FireSky Ranch."

Elizabeth's lips quivered, and her hands trembled. "I don't understand. What's going on?"

"Mom, I've made a ton of mistakes on the ranch, plus sales are down. I'm doing the best I can, but it's not working. We even got a new inmate to stay on the ranch."

Elizabeth leaned back with eyes wide open. "Oh, I didn't know that."

Rick slumped in his chair and focused on the table.

"Have you asked Little Jack and Cassie if they can help? I'm sure they'd want to help keep the ranch."

Rick's head snapped up. "No, and I'd like to keep this between you and me. Asking you for help was hard enough." He pointed to himself. "It was my job to keep FireSky in the family. That will not happen if I don't come up with the money."

Elizabeth pushed her wheelchair away from the table and rolled over next to Rick. "This place is taking everything I've got, so I don't have the money to give you, but I know how you can get it."

"Really? How's that?"

Elizabeth shared her plan. Rick hoped it would work.

Too much was at stake.

Rick was lost in thought as yellow stripes passed below Rusty Red. He had his mom's plan to consider and his explanation to Felicity about the hand delivered package. Was today the right time to share everything with Felicity? The hole he was digging was getting deeper each day he kept her in the dark and he could use her help. How would she react when he got home?

Rick arrived back at the farmhouse and entered the kitchen.

"So what was it?"

Rick stopped. "What was what?"

"The package? What was so important?"

I can't tell her. Not today, but soon.

"Oh, that. It was a late notice on our bank note, but I knew it was coming and already took care of it."

"The note for the ranch and this house?"

"Yes."

"How did that get so far behind they sent a courier to tell you?"

"I said I knew it was coming and have already arranged for the payment."

"What about next month? Is this going to be an ongoing problem?"

Rick sat down at the table.

"Not with the new RIHARP income. It will give us some breathing room."

Felicity put both hands over her face as she shook her head. She exhaled loudly and lowered her hands. "I hope so."

Ten days later, Rick drove to Lone Star Bank with a check for thirty-one thousand dollars to reduce the outstanding balance on his note. He notified the college-age attendant guarding the front door of his intentions. She guided him down the hallway to a different waiting area outside an office with a door plaque that said Kevin Bartolo, Vice President of Collections.

Minutes that felt like weeks later, a skinny man about as tall as James with perfect chestnut brown hair to match his mocha three-piece suit met Rick in the waiting area.

"Mr. Powell, please come into my office."

Rick shared the check and his story. Kevin took the check and jotted notes on a notepad. He affixed them together with a paperclip.

"Will you be calling off the auction now?"

Kevin flashed his charming, professionally whitened smile.

"I'm sorry, Mr. Powell. We require complete repayment of all overdue balances before we can stop a property auction. Unless the delinquent party pays all past-due balances one week before the auction date, we have to proceed."

"Mr. Bartolo, I gave you a check for seventy-five percent of the overdue balance. Doesn't that show a good faith effort I'll pay off the remaining balance?"

Mr. Bartolo tapped several keys on his keyboard.

"You have ten months outstanding. So that—"

"Four months after today," Rick said with his most convincing grin.

The movie star smile appeared again. "We appreciate your efforts, but our policy requires zero past due balances to halt an auction once it's scheduled."

"I get that you have the policy to follow, but our family has been with Lone Star Bank for three decades. Can I get a short extension to pay the past due balance in full?"

Mr. Bartolo crossed his hands and laid them on his desk. "I'm sorry, you're still nearly twelve thousand dollars short. That is the only thing that can stop the auction."

"You've got to be kidding me." Rick stood up and charged out of the office.

He stormed through the lobby and toward the front door. Rick paused long enough to hold the door for an older gentleman. Once the older man was through the door, Rick put his legs into gear and started to exit.

"Are you Wayne Powell's grandson?"

Rick turned around. The older gentleman was talking to him.

"Yes, I am."

"You look just like your dad. I knew you had to be a Powell."

Rick extended his hand. "Thank you, I'm Rick."

"I'm John Moreno. Your grandpa and I go back fifty years when he was just starting the ranch."

"Are you the John Moreno that's a co-founder of Lone Star Bank?"

"Guilty as charged."

"My grandpa always had so much good stuff to say about you. He appreciated everything you did for him. That's why we still do business with Lone Star Bank today."

"That's great, what brings you in today?"

Rick stroked his goatee. "Do you have a minute?"

John looked at his watch. "I have twelve minutes before my next meeting. Will that work?"

Rick nodded.

"Follow me."

Mr. Moreno walked into the nearest open office and shut the door. Rick shared the entire story with Mr. Moreno in less than six minutes.

Mr. Moreno was halfway out the door when he looked to Rick. "I'll be right back."

Four minutes later, Mr. Moreno returned with Mr. Bartolo.

"Mr. Powell, this is Kevin Bartolo. He will assist you with your extension."

Rick sprang up. "Thank you so much, Mr. Moreno."

"Don't thank me, thank your grandfather. He was one of the good guys and I want to see his ranch stay with his family. Please do your best to honor his legacy."

Mr. Bartolo's demeanor changed the next time Rick sat down in his chair. The million-dollar smile never appeared again.

"Well, it seems your family has a long history with Mr. Moreno, so he said to give you another thirty days. It's a one-time extension. You must pay any past-due balance one week before the trustee sale on November tenth, or the auction will take place. No exceptions!"

Rick scurried back to his truck with urgency in his step. He was pardoned today, but the clock was ticking.

CHAPTER TWENTY-SIX

"Mr. Powell, this is Luis. He's our new trainer." Sergio announced.

Rick extended to his hand to the whip-thin man. Luis sprang toward Rick and shook his hand with vigor.

"Welcome to FireSky Ranch Luis. That's quite a grip you've got."

"Thank you, Mr. Powell. Glad to be here."

Rick liked the way he made direct eye contact, and the eager gleam in his eye. Luis was high-energy and clearly a go-getter, just what FireSky needed right now.

Sergio interjected, "Luis has been a trainer for twelve years and can expand the number of lessons we offer, something I know you've wanted to do for a while."

"That's great. I'm looking forward to getting more leases and lesson sign-ups. Again, welcome aboard." Rick turned to Sergio. "Give Luis whatever he needs to get training up to speed as soon as possible."

The new thirty-two-year-old trainer was full of experience and confidence. With Rick's blessing, Luis took control, and made plans to rearrange the tack room and update the pens to suit his plans for the training program.

The diminutive but fiery trainer pushed the FireSky crew very hard. Frustration mounted more and more each day. After several long days repairing the training pen fence and structures in the intense autumn sun, Luis told the crew he wanted to switch the tack room with the supply room, so it was closer to his training pen. Several members of the staff protested, and Luis yelled at them.

James told the rest of the crew, "Don't worry about it, let's just do it."

Luis turned his attention James. "Don't worry about it? Mr. Powell said we need to do whatever it takes to get this place ready for training and I need this."

James stood his ground. "I said don't worry about it; we'll do it."

"Fine, then let's get on it!" Luis barked.

"You don't need to yell."

Luis moved closer to James. "Don't tell me not to yell. I'm doing what I was told, and nobody is helping me."

James walked away.

"Don't walk away from me. You need to get back over here."

James kept walking.

Luis followed him. "This needs to get done today. I said to—"

James whipped around and lifted Luis into the air in one motion. James raised Luis half a foot until his flaring nostrils were inches from the trainer's face.

"Shut up!" James hissed through clenched teeth.

Once James let go of Luis, he dropped to the ground and fell to his side. He was panting like a dog on a hot Texas afternoon. He kept his eyes on James as he sat up and used the stable wall for support.

James backed away from Luis. They rest of the crew watched and huddled together with their mouths open. James gave them a blank look as if he was just as shocked at what just happened.

"I'm telling Sergio about this," Luis said, continuing to back away. "I was following orders."

James bolted.

Sergio found Rick putting boxes into the bed of Rusty Red.

"James left. He took off after a fight with Luis."

"He did what? Where is he? He didn't go into the house, did he?"

"He ran toward the south end."

"We've got to stop him before he sets off Sure Cuffs at the property line."

Rick drove Rusty Red hard until he and Sergio reached the south end. Sergio went right and searched the dense thicket of wild currant. The thorny branches jabbed Sergio's arms and legs with each step deeper in the thicket. He jumped back when a bevy of quail darted from their hidden home.

Rick searched left along Half Moon Creek. He climbed up and down the banks as he followed the creek toward the end of the property.

"Come on James, where are you?"

Rick thought he saw somebody walking in the distance and edged closer to the steep bank to get a better view. The ground gave way and he slid down an embankment twice his height. He punched the soft mud once he came to a stop.

Rick climbed back up, dusting himself off, and continued. He made it to the end of the property and turned around.

Had he misjudged James? James seemed different from Jeff. Calm and cool in the crisis with Blake. Trustworthy, even. But what if he wasn't? What if he was worse than Jeff?

Rick saw Sergio heading toward him.

"I don't see him!" Rick yelled out.

"I don't either. Don't you have a way to track him on your phone?"

"Oh yeah, I do. How could I forget?" Rick tapped the Sure Cuffs app on the screen. "I only have one or two bars here on my phone. I hope this works."

He opened the GPS function and paced around, trying to get a stronger signal. Sergio continued hollering James's name and searching the horizon.

The dot that was James finally appeared on the app. "Found him."

Rick and Sergio studied the screen and calculated that James was about one hundred yards past the grove of trees from where they now stood. James was getting dangerously close to crossing the property line. Once he crossed, it would activate Sure Cuffs and bring an army of law enforcement and TDCJ personnel. James would go back to prison until he completed his sentence.

Did James even know the risk he was taking? How had things gotten so bad so fast that he'd run away?

Rick and Sergio moved with purpose through the dense trees. Rick edged to the front of the two-person single file line. He leapt over dead trees and pushed past branches, wondering if he should call out to James again. A branch he shoved past whipped back and Rick heard Sergio yelp.

"Be careful, those branches can pack a punch," he said.

Rick turned around, "I'm sorry. Are you okay?"

Sergio rubbed his face and then examined his fingers for blood. "Yeah, I'm okay."

"Sorry. He's got to be close to the edge of the property now. We've got to hurry."

Rick lowered his head below the branches and squinted his eyes. He remained still and scanned the edge of the tree line. He saw movement.

"Over there. He's nearly at the property line behind those cedar trees."

He was headed straight toward the neighboring property.

Rick yelled, "James!"

He continued walking.

Sergio and Rick punched through the dense line of saplings and got within ten yards of James.

"James, come back!" Rick pleaded. "You're going to activate Sure Cuffs in a few more feet."

James took a few more steps.

"Please, James. Please stop. We don't want you to go back to prison!"

James froze, but he continued to face the neighbor's pasture.

Rick jogged in front of James, struggling to keep his voice calm. "What's going on, James? Why are you trying to leave the ranch?"

James clenched his jaw and curled his hands into fists.

"I did something stupid."

"What? What did you do that was so stupid?"

James wouldn't look at Rick.

"What did you do?" Rick asked in a tone he'd used when Cody came crying to confess something.

"I— I picked up and pushed the new trainer guy."

"Okay," Rick replied evenly. "Is that it?"

"He said he would tell Sergio we weren't listening to him," James choked. "He said I'd be in trouble."

Rick put his hand on James's shoulder. "When I heard you got into a fight with Luis, I was afraid you beat him up. Fighting each other is not okay, but a little pushing and shoving on a ranch isn't uncommon. You have to try to get along."

James turned to Sergio. "What about Luis?"

"I'll talk to Luis," Sergio assured James.

"You need to take the rest of the day off. We'll start fresh tomorrow."

The journey back to the farmhouse was quiet. Rick checked on James in the rear-view mirror and saw him pinching the skin on his throat, eyebrows drawn, as he stared out the window.

"James, I think we need to let Mrs. Sawyer know about this," Rick said, looking in the mirror for James's reaction.

James locked eyes with Rick in the mirror. He nodded in agreement.

Rick pulled into the parking lot and noticed Cassie's truck. His sister was on the porch talking to Felicity.

As James slinked away to his room, Rick walked toward the porch. "Hey, what's up, Cass?"

"What the heck is going on, Rick?"

Rick flinched. Had she heard about the incident with James? "What?"

"I was going through auction flyers for properties in the area and came across one that looked familiar. It's called FireSky Ranch!"

Rick looked over at Felicity. She leaned back with her arms crossed.

"I thought it was a mistake, so I asked mom if she knew anything about it and she told me you sold the lake house."

"It was my only option."

"How many times have I told you that Jack and I would help you if you needed it? What's wrong with you?"

Cassie stormed inside. Felicity followed her. Rick felt like his feet were stuck in concrete, but knew he had to go inside. He entered the kitchen and leaned against the counter.

Cassie turned in her chair. "You know what's the most disappointing about all this?"

Rick looked at the floor and did not respond.

"I felt sorry for you because I knew how hard you were working to get the ranch on track. I could see the signs that things were not right, and I offered to help you. Many times."

Cassie rose up and moved two feet in front of Rick.

"I would've been happy to help you out if you would've asked or mentioned that you were having problems. Jack would've helped too. We want to save this ranch as much as you do, but you didn't give us an opportunity to help you. Now we no longer have a lake house. You may have had power of attorney, but grandpa always wanted everyone to enjoy this beautiful place. Are you so stubborn that you would have rather let this place go than ask for help?"

Rick crossed his arms tight across his chest. He looked away when their eyes met. He wanted to tell his side of the story, but his voice felt buried deep in his throat.

Cassie started toward the front door. "You break my heart, little brother. Absolutely break it." The door slammed behind her.

Rick turned to Felicity. Surely she'd understand. She'd witnessed his hard work, his struggles to do everything in his power to keep the ranch afloat. But Felicity shook her head and went upstairs.

Rick paced in the kitchen. Disappointing Cassie hurt, but the pain in Felicity's eyes left a deep wound that lingered. Should he tell her everything now? Would it help or make a bad situation even worse?

He dropped into a chair and pounded his fist on the kitchen table. Then he ran his fingers through his hair multiple times. After five minutes of stewing in the kitchen, Rick marched upstairs to the bedroom.

He needed to talk to Felicity. He needed to see her now, so he could explain. She had supported him all this time and he needed to convince her to stay in his corner a little longer until he found a solution.

Felicity was sitting on the bed with her elbows on her knees and her face in her hands. Unsure what to say, Rick froze in the doorway. Maybe he should fill her in about his afternoon adventure. Not the explanation she was probably wanting, but it might break the ice.

"James got into a fight with the new trainer just now and took off. Sergio and I eventually found him and brought him back."

Felicity looked up. Her eyes were red and swollen. Her cheeks were wet with tears.

"How sweet. I'm glad you brought your new asset back to the house, so you can keep receiving RIHARP checks."

It wasn't like her to take a swipe like that. Felicity loved James. No, she was mad about the ranch finances. About his need to look strong when he was anything but. Rick sat down near the foot of the bed.

"I'm sorry. I didn't mean to lie to you."

"We've been arguing a lot the past few months, but I never expected this from you."

Stunned, Rick raised his voice, saying, "Wait a minute, I was only trying—"

Felicity shouted over Rick, "No, *you* wait a minute. You've lied for months about money. You keep saying everything is okay, but it's not."

Felicity glared into Rick's eyes. He looked down. She saw right through him to the wounded kid inside. No woman wanted to be married to a wounded kid. Why did he still feel like the confused boy stuck at fifteen, hoping he was good enough for his daddy?

"You have so many people who are willing to help you. I practically begged you to let me help you, but you shut everybody out. I don't think you realize how much I could help you. You trust nobody but yourself."

Felicity went to the window overlooking the ranch. She put the tips of her fingers over her mouth. Her hand shook. Rick walked up behind her and put his hand on her shoulder. She shrugged it off and stepped away from him.

"I planned to tell you," he said, "but I was waiting for the right time. You seemed so happy. I didn't want to ruin it."

Felicity let out a quick laugh. "Kinda feel foolish now for being so happy. It was all a lie."

"It was never my intention to lie to you or hurt you. I was only trying to protect you."

Felicity spun around, causing Rick to take a step back.

"By lying? By not trusting that I would help you? I don't need a guardian angel, I need a husband. A husband who believes in me. A husband who trusts me."

Felicity grabbed her purse off the dresser and darted down the stairs. She opened the front door, and Rick caught up.

"Where are you going?"

"I don't know. I just know I can't be here right now."

Rick watched Felicity speed away from FireSky Ranch. He

turned toward the kitchen and noticed James standing near the table.

"Everything okay, Mr. Powell?"

"Yeah, just a little argument. It's okay."

Rick hoped that wasn't also a lie.

CHAPTER TWENTY-SEVEN

R ick woke up without an alarm. It was still dark, but he could see the empty space next to him. He got ready and went downstairs. He expected to see James sitting at the kitchen table like every morning.

"I told him last night that we have to get started early today," Rick said aloud. Rocky took this as a sign to follow him.

Rick walked back to James's room, and it was dark. James wasn't in his room or bathroom.

"Oh shoot, I hope he didn't do something stupid again," he muttered, scruffing Rocky's head.

Rick hurried back up the hallway, Rocky's nails clicking along-side him. He checked the powder room and then darted to the family room. He ended up near the front door after checking the entire first floor. James couldn't go upstairs without activating Sure Cuffs, so Rick checked the porch outside.

"Where could he be, Rocky?" he asked the dog, who looked up, tail wagging.

He remembered Sergio's brilliant suggestion down by Half Moon Creek and pulled out his phone. He checked the Sure Cuffs GPS tracker app and found James south of the new stables, and he wasn't moving.

Rick pocketed the phone and departed for the south stable. He wanted to get there before James moved. When Rick neared the south stable, he transitioned into stealth mode. He slowed his stride and crept around the corner. A large silhouette of a man was standing at the edge of the pasture looking up to the sky. Rick tilted his head and squinted.

"James?"

James flinched and turned around.

"Whatcha doing out here?" Rick asked.

James pointed to the east. "I want to see that fire in the sky. I need a fresh start today."

"James, we've got a lot—" Rick caught himself. He put his hands in his pockets and moved closer to James. Rick looked to the east and murmured, "I could use one too."

The two men stood in awed silence as black sky lightened, and the stars disappeared. The back-lit azure sky prepared the world for the coming king of the solar system. Birds sang in anticipation of another blockbuster on the big screen. The sun revealed its radiance while still below the horizon. It painted patches of amber and large swaths of gold in the sky. The colors danced on the blue canvas growing from east to west.

"It looks just like fire in the sky," James muttered without looking away.

Minutes later, the sun sprang up over the eastern hills. The alfalfa seemed to smile once the sun flooded the moist fields with its rays.

"God's showing off today," Rick replied.

James nodded in agreement.

After the sun was in full view in the east, Rick and James walked back to the farmhouse in silence. They ate breakfast and prepared for the day. Before they left the house, Rick texted Felicity and asked if she was okay. She responded that she spent the night at her sister's house north of Austin.

Rick read the eight-word text multiple times looking for clues.

Would she talk to him again? Would she be home soon? Trying to read between the lines was futile, so he gave up.

Rocky started barking and Rick looked through the window. Luis was pulling into the parking lot. Rick rushed outside to meet him at the end of the sidewalk. He planned to apologize for the incident with James.

"Luis, thank you for coming back after what happened yesterday. It'll never happen again."

"I am sure it will never happen again," Luis quickly replied.

Rick took a step back and tilted his head. "I'm glad you're so confident."

"I'm confident because I will not be working here. I wanted to inform you personally."

"Come on Luis, you just started, and we need—"

"My decision is final," Luis interrupted. "I have zero tolerance for crew members acting up when there are plenty of safer places that would appreciate my talents. I've never been physically assaulted like that before. I will not put myself in that position again."

Rick watched Luis—and all the training revenue he could provide—drive away.

The day was long. Rick thought about Felicity as he covered her daily tasks along with his long list of things to do. She made sure every horse got its medicine, supplements, and physical therapy. Felicity had to tend to some of the horses multiple times a day.

Rick crawled into the farmhouse exhausted and ready for dinner. However, dinner wasn't ready for him like he was used to. He couldn't remember the last time he prepared a full meal. He was okay on the grill, but that was about it. He looked in the refrigerator and opened the pantry but couldn't find anything he felt he could make half as well as Felicity.

"I'm sorry about this," Rick said to James as he sat his plate in front of him. It held two plain hot dogs in buns and stale potato chips. "Ketchup and mustard are in the fridge if you need it."

· · ·

For the rest of the week, Rick distracted himself with work. Felicity wouldn't return his calls, but she replied to his texts. Every time Rick heard the ding on his phone and saw it was from Felicity, he straightened up and checked it within a few seconds. Even her two- or three-word responses brightened his day. Rick missed Felicity but knew he had to give her some time. Her wounds were deep, and Rick's dishonesty was the cause. All he could do now was work rebuilding trust between them.

So texts it was for now. Little by little he tried to share more with her.

During a drive back to the ranch, Rick's phone pinged. He snatched his phone off his seat. It wasn't Felicity but someone else he was hoping to hear from, Mrs. Sawyer. After a long apology, she said she would pay a visit to FireSky Ranch the following day. It would be her first stop that morning.

At exactly nine, a maroon Ford Taurus pulled in. Rick greeted Mrs. Sawyer at her car, and they each found a chair on the porch.

"I'm sorry I took so long to get here. We had a lot of new RIHARP transfers last week, so it was a busy, but exciting week."

"That's good news. Would you like something to drink? Water or tea?"

"No, I'm fine, hun. I would like to know what Mr. Edmunds did, though."

Rick shared the story with Mrs. Sawyer. She took notes, nodded and asked several follow-up questions.

"Have you ever seen him act like this before?"

"No, nobody has. Sergio is with him all day on most days and thinks James is a gentle giant."

"I believe he was in the military, wasn't he?" Mrs. Sawyer asked while rifling through pages of a yellow legal pad.

"Yeah, he told us he was in the Army and spent time in Iraq. Why?"

"It's not in his file, but this behavior sounds like it could be caused by PTSD. We see it in so many of our inmates who are veterans. I want to talk to James now, to see if I can learn more. Is that okay?"

"Sure, he's in the kitchen or his room. You know where that is now," Rick said with a laugh.

Twenty minutes later, the screen door clapped behind Mrs. Sawyer as she reappeared on the porch.

Rick put down his phone. "What do you think?"

Mrs. Sawyer sat down next to Rick. "I will have him tested for PTSD. All the signs are there, and we need to treat it right away as part of his rehabilitation."

"Okay. Could you tell me more? Like what should I do to help?"

"If he has PTSD, certain things will trigger a stress response in him. Those reactions could be irrational and even violent. James is in some ways a model prisoner, but until we know more about his triggers, we have to tread lightly. Keep doing what you are doing to give him routine and a sense of safety. Once I have his evaluation scheduled, I'll let you know the date."

After another disappointing microwave meal for lunch, Rick scrolled through his contacts on his phone. He found the number he was looking for and hit send.

"Hello, this is Julia."

"Hey Julia, it's Rick Powell. How's it going? How do you like the new gig?"

"It's great to hear from you. I'm doing well, and the new gig is fine. It's not Longhorn, but it pays the bills. How's it going on the ranch?"

"I'm hanging in there. It has its difficulties like any business."

"You could always start another ad agency. I know a great creative director who would be interested," she teased.

"Don't tempt me."

They both let out a forced, uncomfortable laugh. Rick cleared his throat.

"Julia, I'm hoping that you can help me."

"Sure. What's up?"

"My current advertising is getting horrible click-through rates and I'm spending more each month without getting the conversions I need. It's so hard to concentrate on the creative when you have a hundred other things on your mind. Now I know why companies hired us."

Julia laughed.

"I can't focus on a better design for ads right now so I'm hoping you can work some of your magic and get me a few more eyeballs without breaking the bank."

Julia was quiet for a few seconds, then said, "Yeah. Yeah, I think I can help you out."

Rick and Julia spent a few more minutes on the phone. Julia devised a plan to create video ads for social media using stock footage and target the ads to people living within twenty miles of FireSky Ranch.

Julia shared, "Video is key. It will increase your clicks and lower your cost per click."

"That sounds like a great plan."

"Thanks."

"Julia, you are so good at this. You're a natural. I appreciate you helping me out on this."

"No problem, but before you go, I want to share something with you."

"Sure. Shoot."

"Honestly, I'm not in love with my new job, and if I can't find a better fit here in Austin, I will need to relocate. My old roommate is begging me to come to Chicago and work with her, but I'd rather stay here. If you hear of anything that may be available in Austin, please let me know."

All the oxygen left Rick's chest. A key component of his new agency plan was to hire Julia as his creative director. Losing that option would be a big blow to JWP Agency before it ever got off the ground.

Oxygen returned to his lungs and Rick could respond. "I'm sorry it's not working out. I hope you find a great fit for you in Austin. It would be a crime if the best creative director in Austin left town."

Julia laughed. "Thanks, Rick. I'll get to work on that ad plan for your ranch."

Rick hit the end call button on his phone. He stared at the wall for five minutes before moving again.

CHAPTER TWENTY-EIGHT

J ulia's surprisingly inexpensive plan worked well. A week after they activated the first online ad, Rick received a call from a woman named Brenda. She saw the ad and was looking for a place to board her mustang. They set up an appointment for her to visit FireSky.

The next day, Brenda met Rick near the round pen at Fire Sky Ranch. He walked her around FireSky Ranch and showed her the stables, training pens, wash stalls, and the grazing pasture. Brenda didn't say a word and nodded a lot.

After the tour was over, she spoke. "You have a beautiful ranch here. I'm hoping you can help me. My mother passed away three months ago and left me this mustang."

"I'm sorry," Rick replied.

"Thank you. My mom bought this mustang before she got cancer and she always wanted to ride him. She named him Tolano. He's green, and it would be a new challenge for her, but she never got the chance. They diagnosed her with kidney cancer a few weeks afterward and she passed two years later."

She leaned up against the pen railing.

"My goal is to ride Tolano in honor of my mother. But nobody's ever ridden him. I'll be honest; nobody else will board and train him so I can ride him someday. They say he's too old now to train. You're my last hope."

"I'd like to believe it's never too late for anyone. Everyone deserves a chance."

Brenda and Rick agreed to terms, including a generous training budget. Tolano arrived two days later.

Rick invited everyone into the stall and introduced Sergio, James and the rest of the crew to their new guest.

"Everyone, meet Tolano."

The crew clapped and patted Tolano on his muzzle.

"This guy is a little different. He's four years old but still green, and his owner wants us to help break him so she can ride him."

"But Luis quit. We don't have a trainer," Sergio reminded Rick.

"I know. It's not ideal, but this is a special situation. Tolano was handed down to our client from her mother who passed away three months ago. The owner wants to ride Tolano as a tribute to her late mom, and I said we would do our best."

Nobody said anything.

"Guys, we can do this. All of us ride, and some of us have even broken horses in the past. If we can't do it after giving our best effort, then we can say we did our best. But can we at least give it a shot?"

Heads bobbed up and down.

"Yes, Mr. Powell, we will do our best."

The next day, two members of Sergio's crew tried to get Tolano out of the stall and into a pen. Getting the bridle straps over his ears and the bit in his mouth took over an hour. The crew spent hours with Tolano on activities that should take minutes.

After days of failed attempts to train Tolano, Rick and Sergio leaned against the round pen discussing the next steps.

"I don't know, Mr. Powell; this horse is very stubborn, and wild too long. I don't know if we can do it. Should we hire a real trainer, someone who knows tricks we don't?"

"We can't afford that right now, Sergio. We have to try harder."

"We are trying very hard. This is not an easy horse and trying harder will not work with him."

"I can't give up the lease and training fees right now. We have to find a way to make this work."

"Can I try?" came a voice from behind them.

Rick and Sergio turned around. It was James.

Rick asked, "Do you even know how to ride?"

"I went to camp with my cousin from Houston when I was in high school. We took care of horses and rode them during the summer. I can ride a little."

"That's great, but nobody has ever ridden Tolano, and he doesn't seem to appreciate any attempts to change that. It's a dangerous job and best for someone with more experience."

"I'd still like to try."

Rick looked up into his eyes. He saw no fear — only steely confidence.

"Sergio, what do you think? Is this something we should let James take a shot at?"

"Nothing else is working. If he wants to try it, I say okay."

"Let me think about it."

Rick saw James's face light up.

Sergio excused himself to tend his crew and Rick considered James's strong desire to take on the task of training Tolano. Felicity would know the right thing to do.

Rick typed out a short text to Felicity describing his dilemma with James and desire to talk. He drew in a deep breath and let it out. Rick hit send and glared at his phone for a response. It'd been a week since they talked live, and Rick longed to hear Felicity's voice. After a minute, Rick put his phone in his pocket and headed to the farmhouse.

Ding.

Rick dug his phone out of his pocket in under two seconds.

OK. I'm available now for a few minutes.

Her response was short and oh so sweet to Rick's eyes. He

hurried inside and sat down at the kitchen table, too nervous to stand. He punched in the seven digits and hit send.

When Felicity answered the phone, Rick smiled so wide he could barely speak.

"Hey, how is everything?" He kept his tone breezy, though his heart was hammering.

"It's going okay."

"How's your sister and her family doing?"

"I thought you said this was important." Her voice flared with impatience.

"It is, but I miss you. I think about you all the time, and I wanted to know how you are doing."

Felicity did not respond.

"Okay, I took on a new lease for a horse that's still green. A four-year-old mustang that's never been ridden. The owner received him from her late mother and wanted us to help train him so she can ride him to honor her mother."

"That's sweet."

Rick wasn't sure Felicity was talking about him trying to help someone or the owner wanting to ride a horse in memory of her mother. Based on Felicity's current dissatisfaction for him, he decided it was the latter.

"Yeah, we are trying our best, but this horse wants nothing to do with it. We don't have a trainer...um, Luis didn't work out, and the rest of the crew is getting frustrated."

She sighed heavily. "So what did you call me for?"

"James asked if he could help. I'm not sure if that's a good idea, but he wants to give it a shot, and I don't know what to do. What do you think?"

Felicity's tone softened. "James? Does he know how to train a horse?"

"No, but he's determined, and Sergio says he would let him try."

Felicity was quiet for a few seconds.

"Hello, are you still there?"

"Yes, I'm here. I'm just thinking."

After ten more seconds of silence, Felicity replied, "I think it's worth letting him try. Not to train the horse, but for him and you. He wants to prove he can overcome a major challenge to build confidence and you could use practice trusting somebody other than yourself. It sounds like a good idea."

It was Rick's turn to be silent. He wasn't expecting the jab from Felicity, and it caught him off guard. Rick exhaled into the phone. "Okay, that makes sense."

"Anything else?"

Rick's mind went blank. He had a million things he wanted to tell her, but he couldn't summons the words under pressure. "No, that's it."

Felicity hung up.

Rick looked over at the empty chair that Felicity used to occupy. He took a deep breath and said aloud, "Let's do this."

CHAPTER TWENTY-NINE

Sergio was the first to hear about the Powells' decision to let James work with Tolano. Sergio planned take James through a crash course for the next two days first. Then it would be time to throw him into the deep end of the pool. James had to swim to build confidence.

Next Rick and Sergio shared the news with James. When he heard, he straightened up and smiled so wide they saw the missing tooth.

The next morning, James met Sergio in the new stable, in front of a stall with *Angel* written in chalk on the nameplate affixed to the gate. A buckskin mare with a shiny black mane stood behind the gate waiting to train her next human.

"James, this is Angel. She's the best horse we have on the property to prepare you for Tolano."

James walked up to Angel. He patted her above the nose and Angel took a few steps backward.

"I don't think she likes me."

Sergio laughed. "She's already training you."

"What do you mean?"

"Patience. Training a horse requires patience, knowledge, and understanding. Let a horse get used to you before you touch its face." Sergio demonstrated holding out a palm for Angel to sniff.

Sergio spent the entire day with James. They practiced putting a halter on and off Angel. They did the same with the lunge line. Sergio explained how and when to use the lunge whip in the round pen.

"James, this is called groundwork. That's as far as you'll go when we switch to the green horse. Your goal with Tolano is to pay attention to every detail so you understand him and build trust. Somebody else will train him for a rider, but trust and understanding comes first. Nothing else will work until we understand him and he trusts us."

James smiled and patted Angel between her eyes. She didn't move a muscle.

Sergio spent the next two days training James. James was with Angel from the moment he started his day until he left the stables for bed.

On the third day, Sergio said, "you're as ready as you'll ever be. Tomorrow you'll get started with Tolano. Think about everything Angel taught you and get some sleep tonight. You will need it."

When Sergio arrived the next morning, he saw James standing outside of Tolano's stall. His eyes were fixed on the anxious mustang and he was slowly rubbing his hands together like he was warming them over a fire.

Sergio barked, "What are you waiting for? Get in there."

James fumbled with the gate handle, and when he opened it, Tolano snorted and moved to the back of the stall. When James inched closer with the halter, Tolano spun around in circles, and his hindquarters hit James in the chest. James flew back into the closed gate and fell to the ground. He jumped out of the stall and slammed the gate behind him.

Sergio and the other members of his crew bent over laughing at the comedy in the stall.

"That horse kicked your butt," one of them howled between laughs.

James raised both hands in the air in protest. "What? What's so funny?"

Sergio walked over to James and put his hand on his shoulder. He stopped laughing long enough to say, "I've never seen someone get out of a stall so fast." James joined their laughter, and it broke the tension. He was ready for Tolano now.

The rest of the day, James used his training to build trust with the mustang.

James tiptoed into Tolano's stall the next morning. He turned around to see Sergio and the rest of the staff watching his every move. So he took his time and let Tolano get used to him. When Tolano was ready, he slipped the halter over his ears and secured the straps.

James smiled wide at Sergio and the crew as he walked past them in the stable with Tolano in tow. "See, I've got this."

As soon as Tolano left the shadow of the stall, he reared and kicked with his front hooves. James held onto the lead rope and tried to pull the seven-hundred-pound beast to the round pen, but that only made it worse.

Tolano bucked and spun again as he did in the stall. This time James caught a back hoof right above his knee. James let go of the rope and collapsed in a heap, yelping in pain.

Sergio ran over to James, and the rest of the crew herded Tolano into the pen.

"Are you okay?"

James rubbed his quad while gritting his teeth.

"Yeah. He caught me good, though."

"Can you walk?"

"Just give me a minute."

James nursed his new softball-size bruise while Sergio returned Tolano to his stall. Sergio gave James the rest of the day off to recover.

He told Rick about the incident as he was leaving the ranch.

Rick said he would come tomorrow to observe James and his battle with Tolano.

The next day started like Sergio's description of the previous one. Only this time, James got Tolano into the round pen for his groundwork before he acted up, which seemed like a good sign to Rick. But James had to jump over the fence three times to avoid flying hooves.

"You still sure you want to do this?" Rick asked.

"I'm sure, Mr. Powell. I'm breaking this horse. He ain't breaking me."

"I'll double check the TDCJ health insurance plan to make sure it's all paid up."

James waved Rick off and continued to focus on Tolano.

After an hour, Tolano was cantering around the pen with James in the middle guiding him. James was getting the upper hand. This trend continued for several days until James could take Tolano to the pen for groundwork without incident. It impressed Rick. They still had to train Tolano to accept a rider, but James made more progress than Rick thought he would.

Rick finished his feed order early and dropped in on James and Tolano. He spotted James brushing Tolano, talking to the animal. Rick slowed his steps and inched closer. He dropped down behind a stall wall. James spoke to Tolano in a deep, soothing voice. Rick couldn't believe how calm the once-wild mustang was with him, patiently accepting the grooming without flinching or shying.

"It's just like I told ya, buddy. People don't understand us. We're complicated. They don't know why we do what we do, but I get you. We're alike, so we need to stick together. That's right; we need to stick together. It's you and me, boy. We're a team, and we're in this together."

When James finished brushing Tolano's right side, he crossed in front of the horse to work on his left side.

Rick received a text, and the notification ping sounded like a giant alarm bell. He dove behind another stall door, listening for sounds of Tolano spooking. But the only noise was the steady sweep of the brush against Tolano's coat. Rick wiped his brow and looked to see who texted him. It was a message from Mrs. Sawyer saying she'd scheduled a medical team from TDCJ to test James tomorrow.

Rick came out of his hiding spot to tell James he wouldn't be training Tolano tomorrow, because there was an important task he would be needed for. James nodded sadly, and stayed late with the mustang.

The bedroom was darker than the previous mornings. A steady rain lingered after an early thunderstorm. Down in the kitchen over coffee, Rick shared the news of the PTSD test with James. Rick studied James's face as he processed the news. He still couldn't read James after all their time together.

The rain stopped, but the air was thick. Mrs. Sawyer and her maroon Ford pulled in first. A black GMC Yukon SUV followed her in the parking lot. Rick commanded Rocky to retreat to the porch, then he led Mrs. Sawyer and her two colleagues to the family room.

"Mr. Powell, this is Dr. Von Hoft. He's the clinical psychologist for the Texas Department of Criminal Justice."

Rick shook hands with the gentleman in his mid-fifties who positioned his wire-rim glasses at the top of his pointy nose and below his clean-shaven head. "Nice to meet you, doctor," Rick responded.

A young man in his thirties stood next to Dr. Von Hoft. "Hello, Mr. Powell, I'm Chad Jeffries. I'm the PA who will assist Dr. Von Hoft today." He had a firm handshake and a high and tight haircut. Rick guessed he was former military.

The two men put their briefcases on the coffee table while Mrs. Sawyer explained the process to Rick. "This will take two hours.

They'll conduct tests, but most of all they want to get to know James. Are you okay leaving us here alone during the evaluation?"

"Sure, I've got plenty to do on the ranch. You've got my number if you need me."

Rick helped Sergio's team load a mare in the south end. They secured her in a trailer, and one of Sergio's guys drove to a new veterinarian in Travis County. Rick couldn't afford an on-site visit from a vet anymore.

The crew remained in the south end and cut branches along the riding trail from the stables to Half Moon Creek to make it safe for their future guests.

"Sergio, I've got to get back to the house, but keep the crew on this trail until it's cleaned up. I'm going to restart the walking trail rides again for the little kids. It will bring in some revenue while we try to find a new trainer now that Luis is gone."

Sergio adjusted his hat and smiled. "That's a good idea, Mr. Powell. I remember we had a waiting list when we used to take those kiddos out years ago."

"It got to be too much for my mom to manage after grandpa died, but I think we can do it again. After we make the trail safe, we'll need to refurbish the old gear for young riders. I think we still have some of the small Western saddles in the loft above the tack room."

"I've seen them recently, Mr. Powell. We'll pull them out and clean them all up."

When Rick arrived back at the stables, he realized he had been away from the house for over two hours. He passed sixteen stalls and peeked through the open doors. Dr. Von Hoft, Mr. Jeffries, and Mrs. Sawyer were gathering on the porch.

Rick headed over to meet them. When he reached the top porch step, he heard, "Mr. Powell, please have a seat."

Rick sat on the wicker couch next to Mrs. Sawyer. He leaned forward with his forearms resting on his thighs. Dr. Von Hoft positioned a chair across from of Rick.

"Mr. Edmunds has PTSD. He sustained trauma in Iraq, including witnessing an IED blast that killed a guy in his squad. He has nightmares several nights a week. It's severe."

Rick leaned back into the cranberry red cushion and exhaled. "I had a feeling."

Mrs. Sawyer put her hand on Rick's knee. "This is an official diagnosis. He'll get the help he needs now." She explained the course of treatment that included regular visits with a therapist.

Rick moved to the edge of his seat. "What do I do now?"

Mrs. Sawyer turned to Dr. Von Hoft, and he answered, "Every case of PTSD is different, so we don't know for sure now what will trigger him. Treat him like you have so far—routine is very important for James, knowing what to expect. Try to avoid high-stress and chaotic situations."

"Could he be violent if something triggers him?"

"It's possible," Dr. Von Hoft replied without breaking eye contact with Rick.

Rick leaned back again and interlocked his fingers behind his head. He exhaled and jumped up, "I can do this. I'll do my best to keep him out of stressful situations and make sure he's available for all his therapy sessions."

After both vehicles left, Rick sank back into a chair on the porch and shook his head. His heartbeat increased when he thought about Felicity living with her sister and James with PTSD. He could snap, and he'd committed murder once. "I can't believe this is happening."

The cell phone buzzed in Rick's front pocket. Rick saw Julia's name appear on the screen and answered after two rings.

"Hey Rick, how's it going?"

"Not good."

"What happened? Is everyone okay?"

"Yeah, everyone is okay. I'm just having a bad day. Could I tell you about it over coffee?"

Julia cleared her throat. "That's why I'm calling you. I can't meet up for coffee next week."

"That's fine. We can reschedule for another time."

"I'm moving to Chicago."

Rick felt the oxygen leave his lungs, and the porch started to spin. His critical asset to launching the JWP Agency was leaving. JWP was slipping far, far away. The spinning grew worse. Rick clicked to end the call while Julia was still talking.

He leaned on the door jamb to get into the house and took several large steps to the bathroom. Once in the bathroom, he dry heaved for a minute and sat down next to the toilet. Rick wiped his mouth and flushed the toilet. His dream for JWP swirled in the bowl and vanished.

CHAPTER THIRTY

Rick started a fire in the fire pit. Once it was burning well, he marched into the kitchen.

"Fire's ready if you want to…."

The empty chair stabbed Rick's eyes like daggers. He dropped his head in defeat.

"What's that?" James yelled from his room.

Rick sighed and leaned against the door frame. A silhouette of James appeared in the guest suite doorway. "Nothing."

Rick turned back to the fire pit and stopped. The silhouette vanished.

"You want to join me by the fire?" Rick shouted down the hallway. "I've got a big bag of delicious cheddar coated popcorn that I can't eat by myself."

"Okay. Sure."

Both men settled in chairs. They ate popcorn and listened to the crickets sing their love songs. Rick and James watched the flames dance for a half hour without saying a word.

James spoke first. "You want to know what I did to end up in prison?"

Rick sat up straight and leaned toward James. "Yeah. If you're ready."

"I'm ready."

James put his hands in his coat pockets and stared deep into the fire. He cleared this throat.

"I was with my little brother Jonathan at a bar just a few miles from our house. We were hanging out, and we both had a little too much to drink. I look over, and Jonathan is talking to this smokin' sister. We didn't know her boyfriend was on the other side of the bar and when he returned, things got heated. The bartender pulled out a bat and told them both to take it outside. Jonathan and me never backed down from any beef, so we went outside."

Rick's eyes widened, fearing what would come next.

James talked faster. "Once we get outside, they start talking smack and shoving each other. Then this dude sucker punches Jonathan. Jonathan popped up like he was shot out of a cannon and pulled out his Glock. I didn't know he even had it. Before Jonathan could even get off a shot, the other guy popped him in the stomach."

James stood up and gestured wildly while he continued.

"I looked down and saw Jonathan bleeding on the ground. My little brother was lying in a pool of his own blood. Something inside me snapped. I saw the other guy take off and noticed the Glock lying next to Jonathan on the ground. I picked it up and started after the guy who shot my brother. He hopped in a car with another guy and tore out of the parking lot. I wasn't even thinking. I unloaded a full magazine into the rear window of the car and hit them both."

James extended his arm as if he was shooting at them now. He noticed and dropped his arm. He sat down, took a deep breath and slowed his pace.

"The car pulled over alongside the road and some people in the parking lot called 911. The driver survived with a shoulder injury. But the other guy, the one who shot my brother, I hit twice: once in his upper arm and another time in his neck. I guess the bullet hit an artery. He was bleeding bad and died before the ambulance arrived. I was in shock. I stood in the same place until the police arrived."

James took a deep breath and continued, "the police put me in handcuffs and walked me to the ambulance where they were loading my brother. He was unconscious, and I was scared I'd never see him again, but he lived. Paralyzed from the waist down. He's in a wheelchair today."

James turned his attention back to the flickering flames.

"When I went to trial, my attorney said I should take a plea deal for seven years. I never did anything wrong, so I pleaded self-defense. The jury didn't seem to care that I wouldn't have shot that guy if he hadn't shot my brother first. I was defending myself and my brother, but they thought since I chased him, it was second-degree murder. They gave me the max, twenty-two years in prison. I still don't know why they found me guilty of second-degree murder. It wasn't planned or anything. I was just reacting to my brother getting shot by some guy who started a fight. I didn't do anything wrong."

It was silent around the fire pit for several minutes. Rick looked over at the trance-like look on James's face and broke the silence. "You still feel that way?"

"What way?"

"Like you did nothing wrong."

"I didn't."

Rick cleared his throat. He tried to talk for a split second and stopped himself. After another minute of consideration, Rick blurted out, "I know you will not like hearing this James, but I think you need to take some accountability for what happened. I think you have a legitimate beef with your lawyer, your sentence, and that you have PTSD, but you pulled the trigger. Another man is dead because of what you did, even if that wasn't your intention."

"Mr. Powell, you don't know me or everything else that happened."

"You're right, but I know about accepting responsibility. I know the importance of forgiveness."

"How do you know about forgiveness? You've got this big family ranch. A wife and kids."

Rick chuckled. "It may seem rosy from the outside, but I've got a dogfight going on inside me." He got up and put another log on the fire. "How do I know about forgiveness? Do you really want to know?"

James stared at Rick.

"Well, a drunk driver killed my dad when I was fifteen and the guy who did it was in prison less than eight years. He never apologized or asked for forgiveness. It still bothers me. I don't think he was sorry for what he did." Rick looked at James. "Are you at all sorry for what you did?"

"I was protecting my brother."

Rick could hear the agitation in his voice, and he remembered his conversation with Dr. Von Hoft earlier in the week. He didn't want to create stress and trigger anything in James. Rick stopped pressing the conversation. They turned their attention to the dancing flames and the flickering embers.

After a few minutes, Rick shared his final thoughts.

"James, my whole point is that you will get a second chance so that you can start the healing process now. Take care of your PTSD and seek forgiveness for what you've done. It won't be just for them, but good for you, too."

Neither spoke again until James got up, saying, "I'm going to bed."

Rick sunk deep into his chair and stared at the red embers until they turned black.

CHAPTER THIRTY-ONE

The second serving of piping-hot black goodness filled Rick's mug just below the rim. He let the warmth soothe his throat as he watched James working with the mustang in the round pen. Rick left the farmhouse to find Sergio in the tack room.

"Has James been acting normal to you the last few weeks?"

Sergio threw a saddle blanket onto the middle shelf. He tilted his head and examined the support beam in the middle of the room.

"Hmm. Now that you mention it, he has been quieter than normal. I've also seen him get frustrated more often during the last few days. He's typically even keel."

"I know. I'm wondering if his PTSD is acting up. Let me reach out to his counselor and see what she says."

Rick pulled out his phone, scrolled through his contact list and put through a call to Mrs. Sawyer.

Once they exchanged pleasantries, Rick got to the point. "James is acting different. He's quieter than normal, and Sergio says he gets frustrated faster since the PTSD diagnosis. But I don't think he's under any stress."

Rick could hear her typing in his ear. The typing stopped. "It could be depression. Sometimes treatment for PTSD will have that effect on people. I have an opening tomorrow, so I can pop out there to see him."

When Mrs. Sawyer arrived the next day, Rick suggested they talk on the porch. Once they found a comfortable seat, Mrs. Sawyer asked Rick to share more about James's behavior.

"He was doing well, in fact, better than I expected. However, we had a long talk around the fire recently, and he shared the details about his crime. He told me he thought he was a victim and got a bad deal. I shared how I lost my father to a drunk driver. I guess I'm still defensive about owning the harm done to others, regardless of intention, because, well... I told him he should take accountability for what he did. Looking back, I should have shown him more grace since he was honest with me. Plus, he's struggling with PTSD. He just pushed a hot button for me. Do you think maybe I'm the cause of his bad mood?"

"Mr. Powell, I'm sorry for your loss. You did nothing wrong. Let me talk to him and see how he's doing."

"He's in his bedroom right now."

Mrs. Sawyer spent over an hour in the guest suite with James. After forty-five minutes, Rick paced like an expectant father in the waiting room, eyes glued to the bedroom door. When it finally opened, it was all he could do to not pounce on Mrs. Sawyer to get news.

"I'm glad you called, Mr. Powell. James has a lot on in his mind. He took what you said to heart, and he's struggling with it."

"I'm sorry. I didn't mean to trigger anything with him."

"It's okay. It's good he's considering a different perspective on what he did. Although it's a painful process to go through, admitting he did something wrong is an essential step toward rehabilitation. The goal is for James to forgive the victim's family. James still believes he was in the right and that they helped send him to prison for twenty years. He feels they owe him and he'll never let go of the bitterness until he forgives them. Cancels their debt to him."

Rick took a few steps and leaned against the porch support post and railing. "You sound like my pastor."

"Your pastor sounds like a smart person. Has he taught you Matthew 6:14?"

"I'm not sure. What's it say?"

"It says, 'if you forgive other people when they sin against you, your heavenly Father will also forgive you.'"

Rick nodded.

Images of his brother filled Rick's mind. He'd wondered many times in the past how he could have a strong relationship with Jack. Could apologizing be the answer?

Rick shook off those feelings and leaned over the railing. He gazed over FireSky Ranch. "I just figured James needed to say he was sorry to the victim's family. But there's more to it than I thought. He seems bitter about the whole situation."

Mrs. Sawyer moved closer to Rick. "It's hard for inmates to say they're sorry and forgive others who may have hurt them. They see it as a sign of weakness or letting someone get away with something. People outside of prison like you and me do it all the time. People hurt us and instead of holding onto the bitterness forever, we forgive them. Not for their benefit, but for ours. I hope that James can get to that point."

Rick crossed his arms. "Is it that important for James to overcome his bitterness? Shouldn't he focus on his PTSD treatment and good behavior so he can get out of prison?"

"Bitterness is a prison."

Mrs. Sawyer's answer clung to Rick like an infant to its mother. It pushed out every other conscious thought in his brain and Rick could not respond.

Mrs. Sawyer moved to the railing. She joined Rick in his gaze over FireSky. "This place is good for James. He will go through some tough days, but he's learning valuable skills here that he couldn't get in many other places. He'll be more prepared after he's out of the prison system because of this experience. Keep up the good work, Mr. Powell."

Rick needed to hear those words. He walked Mrs. Sawyer back to her car and thanked her for coming on such short notice. Rick skipped back to the house and bounced into the kitchen with a wide smile. The empty kitchen hit him like a punch in the gut.

Rick's smile disappeared. He couldn't share the good report from Mrs. Sawyer with Felicity. The sting of her absence grew more painful each day. He couldn't be in that room anymore. He needed to get away.

Rick thought of his mom, her way of listening so you felt heard and understood. He could visit her, and she might have good advice for him. She's dealt with Powell men for five decades and seemed to like them still. Most of the time.

As soon as Rick saw Elizabeth in the game room, her pale lips and droopy eyelids caught his attention. He kissed her on the forehead and sat down next to her at a game table.

"How ya feeling, Mom?"

"Oh, not too good. My blood pressure has been rising again, so they gave me stronger medicine. I haven't felt well since I started the higher dose."

"Does the nurse know you're not feeling so good?"

"Yeah, she knows. She thinks I may also have a touch of a cold, so she wants to give it a few more days."

"Stay on her, Ma."

Elizabeth pushed a deck of cards over to Rick.

"I think a game of rummy would make me feel better."

"Pulling the sick card to get me to play rummy. How could I resist?" Rick laughed and shuffled the cards.

Rick and Elizabeth played two games of rummy. Rick didn't put up too much resistance, and Elizabeth cruised to win both games. He never mentioned Felicity but asked her a question that had been weighing on him.

"Mom, I'm struggling to turn FireSky around. I'm not sure I can do it, and I don't think Cassie or Jack would leave their careers."

Elizabeth put down the cards and gave Rick her full attention.

"I know it's preferred for a Powell to run FireSky, but that may not always be possible. Could you trust someone else to lead FireSky Ranch?"

Elizabeth looked down at her hands folded on top of the table. She didn't respond for a few seconds and Rick felt the acid churning in his stomach. He didn't mean to ask her today when she wasn't feeling well. Now Rick may have pushed her too far.

She reached over and grabbed Rick's hand.

"I'm sorry if I ever gave you the impression that only a member of the Powell family could manage FireSky."

Rick put his hand on top of his mother's hand.

"Of course, we could trust the right person or people to run the ranch. Your father and grandfather were very trusting of others. They liked to give people a chance. One chance to prove themselves and another chance to redeem themselves if they screwed up the first time. They believed in second chances. Sometimes they gave multiple second chances."

Elizabeth coughed. She pulled a handkerchief out of her sweater pocket and held it over her mouth until she stopped coughing.

"Some of our richest relationships and business partners, like Sergio, came from taking a chance on somebody without Powell blood. Don't be afraid to ask for help from anyone who can and will help you."

Rick nodded in agreement and Elizabeth pushed herself away from the table.

"I'm sorry, but I'm exhausted. Can you help me to my room? I may need a nap."

After Rick helped Elizabeth out of her wheelchair and on to her bed, he said, "thank you for all the great advice. You've given me a lot to think about."

Elizabeth smiled as she laid her head back onto her fluffy pillow. "Thanks for being brave enough to play rummy with me. I enjoyed it."

Rick closed the door slowly. He didn't like the way she looked as she closed her eyes.

CHAPTER THIRTY-TWO

Rick woke up early but stayed in bed. He couldn't stop thinking about Felicity and how much he hurt her. Rick knew he'd never do it again, but he had to convince Felicity to give him a second chance. That wouldn't be easy. She wouldn't see him right now.

He grabbed his phone from his nightstand and tapped out a few sentences. After looking at the message for a minute, Rick hit the delete button multiple times until the message vanished. He tossed the phone back on the nightstand. Five seconds later he picked it back up again. Rick typed out another lengthy message to Felicity expressing sincere regret for his behavior. The message included a request for Felicity to meet at her favorite restaurant in Austin for dinner that evening. He stared at the characters and read the message a half dozen times. Rick's finger hovered over the delete button, but instead hit send. He threw the phone onto Felicity's side of the bed and buried his head under a pillow.

Rick agonized over the content of his text. He continued to rewrite the message in his head with more convincing prose.

Ding!

He dug through the covers until he found his phone. It contained a two-letter response: *OK*.

Rick leaped out of bed. The countdown to see Felicity began.

It was the shortest day Rick could remember. His mind was on the message he'd deliver to Felicity at dinner. He wanted her to come back home. How could he bring it up? Talk about James first or jump right in? Rick wiped his sweaty hands on his pants and looked at his watch. He wanted to be on time, so he rushed through his many tasks so he could quit early.

Rick left ninety minutes early for the forty-five-minute drive to downtown Austin. He parked in a nearby parking garage and walked to the Roaring Fork.

Thoughts of Felicity flooded his mind as soon as he entered the building. For the past decade, The Roaring Fork was his wife's favorite restaurant. The restaurant's familiar sights, sounds, and smells brought back memories of birthdays and anniversaries. Rick secured a seat in the lounge with an unobstructed view of the front door, so he could see Felicity when she arrived.

Twenty minutes later, Felicity appeared in the waiting area of Roaring Fork. She was in a black, knee-length dress with the hair framing her face pulled into a clip on top of her head and the back loosely floating around her shoulders. She stood out like a movie star on the red carpet. Rick's mouth fell open as he watched Felicity speak to the host.

He closed his mouth and strolled to the host stand to meet his wife.

An awkward silence filled the air between Felicity and Rick as they looked each other over. It felt like a first date. Felicity clung to her small purse, and Rick twisted his keys in his pant pocket.

The hostess saved them from enduring more awkwardness by announcing, "Powell party of two."

Rick pulled out Felicity's chair for her, and then sat across from her. Felicity placed her purse on the table and Rick opened the menu to the appetizers section. The silence grew uncomfortable.

Rick convinced himself to speak. "Did Cody tell you he may get a promotion soon?"

They both exhaled and let out a nervous laugh.

"Yes, he told me a couple of days ago. That's exciting since he hasn't been there very long."

They made small talk about the kids as they placed their order for drinks and then their main course. As the server was leaving, Rick added one more item.

"Please bring an order of the green chile mac and cheese as an appetizer."

"You remembered? That's my favorite."

"Of course, I did."

After taking a sip of water and buttering a roll, Felicity scanned the room. She had a sheepish grin on her face.

"What's so funny?" Rick asked.

"Nothing."

"No, tell me. I could use a laugh, too," Rick said with a smile of his own.

"Okay, it's not funny, but I've been thinking about FireSky, and I have a good idea. At least I think it's good."

"You've been thinking about FireSky? What is it?"

Rick wasn't sure what Felicity had planned for their future but did a gentle fist pump under the table.

"What about adding chickens for eggs and a small garden for vegetables behind the new stable? We could sell the eggs and veggies."

"Not bad, but FireSky has always been about boarding, training, and riding horses. I'm not so sure chickens and veggies are a fit."

"FireSky has always been about educating and training people. Horses were the tool. I think it's a logical extension. Kids can care for chickens, grow veggies, and learn responsibility. There are kids in Austin who never get to put their fingers in the dirt."

"Hmmm. That is a pretty good idea."

Rick stroked his goatee as he thought about the proposal. He thought more about the fact that Felicity sounded like she was open to coming back to FireSky Ranch.

The server arrived with Felicity's appetizer. While she ate, Rick spoke up. "The RIHARP counselor stopped by the other day. Ever since the PTSD diagnosis, James has not been himself. But he has opened up to me." Rick shared a condensed version of James's story of the bar fight that led to his prison sentence.

Felicity leaned in and listened to every word. She nodded occasionally and was silent until Rick finished.

"That explains a lot," Felicity whispered as she continued to stare straight ahead. "I'm glad he was able to share with you."

"I was too, but I wasn't sure what to say after he told me the story." Rick shifted in his seat and took a sip of his drink.

Their main entrees arrived, giving Rick a moment to collect his thoughts.

"I told him he should seek forgiveness from the victim's family," Rick continued, "but James doesn't think he did anything wrong. I told him he should take responsibility for his actions. During our talk, I told him about my dad and how much it would have helped me to hear an apology. James has been acting funny ever since. Mrs. Sawyer said it's positive for him to consider a new perspective on his role in the crime."

"That seems like good advice. I'm sure your vulnerability and honesty struck a chord with him." Felicity replied with a faint smile.

Rick wasn't sure how to respond. He was tired of hiding his feelings from his wife.

"Maybe. He is quieter than normal and seems agitated more often. I may have triggered his PTSD, or I may have been too direct."

Rick downed a third of his glass of water and cleared his throat.

"Speaking of being direct, would you come back home?"

Felicity put down her fork and leaned back in her chair. She tilted her head and looked at Rick but did not respond.

Rick kept selling. "It would help James if you could talk to him. He needs help to get on the right path, and I know you'll do a much better job than me. Plus, we need you back at the ranch. Sergio, me, and the rest of the crew combined can't replace what you did on FireSky."

"I don't know about that. What about us? Can you be honest with me going forward?"

Rick placed his napkin next to his plate and lowered his eyes to the table. He knew he had to be one hundred percent honest with Felicity. He looked up and let it all out.

"Yes, I can. I'll never lie to you again. I have to tell you something important, so you'll know everything about the ranch finances."

Rick paused as the server removed the empty plates. Once he was out of earshot, he continued.

"You know how I sold the lake house to some investors to stop the auction?"

"I didn't know who bought it, but yeah, I won't forget that conversation."

"Well, I needed money fast, so I sold to one of those cash-for-homes companies, but it wasn't enough to pay off all the debt."

Rick's voice trailed off. He looked down at his hands and opened his mouth. His words stuck in his throat.

"So?"

"It delayed the auction. I need to come up with another twelve thousand dollars in three weeks or the auction for FireSky will continue."

"What are you going to do? What's your plan?"

"I don't know. I don't have one yet."

"Rick, I can't believe you let it get that bad. We may lose everything."

Rick looked down at the white table cloth between him and

Felicity, "I know. It's not easy to admit that I've made mistakes, but I said I would be completely honest with you."

Felicity pushed away from the table.

"I appreciate your honesty, but it's a lot to take in. I need some time to think about all this."

Rick stood up, "will you come back to the ranch so we can work this out together?"

"Not tonight. Good night, Rick."

Rick watched Felicity pass through the front door and disappear.

CHAPTER THIRTY-THREE

The next morning, Rick toured the grounds at FireSky. Felicity had stirred his resolve to avoid the auction and save the ranch. Decades of materials and equipment gathered on the west side of the old stable. By design, it wasn't noticeable from the farmhouse or the parking lot.

Much of the heap behind the stable belonged in the dump. However, some of it was not only salvageable but valuable. The crown jewel was a John Deere 5103 utility tractor. It looked sad after sitting uncovered for the last year, but was less than fifteen years old and still ran well despite being uglier than the new five series John Deere Rick purchased a year ago. The new tractor was fully financed, so Rick couldn't sell it.

The old utility tractor could likely fetch eighty percent of the twelve thousand dollars Rick owed to cancel the auction. He had to clean it up good, though. He also found a tiller and mower attachment along with a large stack of unused fencing materials— valuable items on any ranch in Hays County.

Rick went inside the supply room and found an entire shelf full of old saddles and equestrian tools. He calculated a reasonable price to sell each item and added everything up. If he sold everything, he could generate over fifteen thousand dollars. He smiled at the prospect.

Rick raced to locate Sergio and asked him to call the team together for a meeting. The small crew of seven assembled on the west side of the old stable. Rick addressed the team, "I'm having a ranch sale on November second to get rid of all this stuff. There is more inside the supply room inside. Everything needs to be cleaned up and put in good working order so we can sell for top dollar. If we don't, I'll have to make major cuts to everything on this ranch. I'd have to let some of you go, which I don't want to do. You're an amazing team and I value every single one of you. You're much more important than stuff."

Rick moved a couple steps closer to the team.

"It's October sixteenth, and we have less than three weeks to get everything ready to for a sale. I've also provided Sergio with plans to build chicken coops behind the south stable and create a garden, starting with cool-weather crops. We need to get all this done along with our regular duties on the ranch. It's a lot to do in a short amount of time, so I hope I can count on everyone to help meet that deadline."

Rick looked to the crews and saw nodding heads, except for one.

"Lucas, are you with us?"

A young man in his late twenties stood up with a pained look. He shook his head, "No, Mr. Powell, I can't join you. My daughter is sick and will be in the hospital a lot. My wife is working for our health benefits, so I need to work less, not more. My little girl is two and I need to focus on her until she's better."

Rick stared at Lucas. He could feel all the eyes of the team on him, waiting for his response. Rick walked over to Lucas and put his hand on his shoulder. "I'm sorry about your daughter. I wish I could help more, but I can't right now, so do what you need to do. If everything works out here like I expect, the door to come back at FireSky is open for you to return."

The young man smiled, and Rick gave him a gentle nudge. "Go on, get home to your daughter now."

The team watched Lucas grab his belongings and head to his car.

Rick turned back to the team and saw the lowered eyes and straight lips. "This is only going to get harder now without Lucas. Does anyone else want or need to leave?"

Nobody spoke for several seconds. Sergio stepped forward and said, "Mr. Powell, we are ready for the challenge. You have the full support of the team."

"Great. I appreciate all of your help on this. Sergio, I'll need your best guy at fixing equipment to get on the utility tractor right away. You have to lead the charge on everything else."

"Will do, Mr. Powell."

"Alex, you've got the utility tractor," Sergio said. "Everyone else, follow me." He waved to the team and they marched toward the supply room.

Rick created ads for all the local bulletin boards and placed others online. He wanted to sell everything. Two days later, they moved everything planned for the sale into the equipment barn. Dusty, unused equipment was coming back to life and eager for a new owner. He reached the John Deere utility tractor and found Alex changing the oil underneath.

Rick leaned up against the dusty tire. "Keep up the good work, Alex."

Rick's phone buzzed. It was Cassie.

"Hey, Cass, what's up?"

"Rick, you need to get down to Saint David Medical Center as soon as possible. Gentle Breeze called, and they think mom had another stroke. The ambulance left a few minutes ago so she should be there soon. I'll be there as soon as I can."

"I'm leaving right now."

Rick found Sergio. "I've gotta go now. My mom is at Saint David's, so I'll call you later to let you know what's going on."

Rick changed into clean clothes and jumped into Rusty Red.

He twisted the key, and the engine tried to turn over but wouldn't start. He tried three more times. Rick slammed his fist on the dash and yelled, "Not today!"

Rick sat in the driver's seat and took a deep breath. He prayed a prayer well-known to owners of old trucks: "God, I need this truck to start. Please let it start one more time."

He rubbed his hands together and turned the key. The engine turned over again, but this time it made a sputtering noise as the pistons turned.

"Thank you, God. Now please let my mom be okay."

Elizabeth was in a room in the Intensive Care wing of the medical center. Cassie was already next to her bed.

The beeps of the monitors and Elizabeth's motionless body were the first things Rick noticed. He walked up next to Cassie as she stood by the side of the bed.

"How is she?"

"Not good. She's still unconscious. They're sure she had another stroke."

"She said she wasn't feeling too well when I stopped by last week. I think she sensed something wasn't right."

Cassie sat down in the chair and put her hands over her face.

"They need to run more tests, so I guess we have to wait and see how bad it was this time."

"Did you already call Jack?" Rick inquired.

"Yes, he'll try to get here later today."

Later that afternoon, Cassie's and Rick's families were in the Saint David ICU waiting room. Jack Jr. was on his way from Kansas City. It was a familiar scene from a little over a year ago after Elizabeth's first stroke, but this one had a more ominous prognosis. The doctors told the family that Elizabeth had a major stroke and was in a coma. They weren't sure if she had the strength to recover.

Felicity was in the waiting room. Her presence helped ease the sting of Rick's ill mother. Seeing her with Cody, McKenna, and the other Powells made Rick appreciate her even more. They made small talk in the waiting room as they waited for their turns to have brief visits with Elizabeth.

Rick stayed at the hospital all night and well into the following day. The plight of FireSky was still heavy on his mind and he wanted to give Sergio and James direction on the final preparations for the sale. Not wanting to leave Elizabeth's side, he asked Felicity if she would go to the cafeteria with him for a quick conversation. She agreed.

"Thanks for all your support of my mom and the rest of the family. It means a lot to me for you to be here."

"Of course, I would be here. I've known Elizabeth for twenty-five years."

Rick took a long sip from his steaming cup of coffee.

"I have a favor to ask you."

Felicity crossed her arms and legs. "Okay, what is it?"

"Could you please go back to FireSky and give Sergio an update on Elizabeth? I don't want to leave, and I don't know when I'll get back. I want someone to let Sergio know what's going on here."

Felicity flashed a quick smile and stood. "Sure. I'll go before he leaves for the day."

"I have one more thing."

Felicity paused for a second and then sat back down.

"Please talk to James. I'm concerned about him. Mrs. Sawyer talked to him for a while last week. She thought his depression was a normal part of him taking responsibility for his crime. I'm not so sure how he feels about me, but I know he respects you. He may open up to you if he sees you back on the ranch. You may be able to help him figure out whatever is bothering him."

Felicity nodded several times. "Poor guy. Yeah, I'll talk to James and see what's on his mind."

"Thank you. I appreciate your help."

Felicity gave Rick's hand a quick squeeze followed by a smile. "I'll see you later."

After Felicity told Sergio about Elizabeth, she went back up to the porch. She saw James walking from the stables into the farmhouse. Each step was slow and measured, his eyes fixed on the ground.

"Would you like some iced tea?"

James turned to the porch. "Yes, Mrs. Powell, thank you very much."

Felicity put two glasses of iced tea down on the wicker coffee table.

"I haven't had a chance to talk to you in weeks. How are things going for you?"

"Okay, I guess. Did Mr. Powell tell you that the counselor came here because I'm confused right now?"

"He did. What's troubling you?"

"Been thinking about what I did. I feel bad for the other family that lost their son. I want to tell them I'm sorry for what I did, but I don't know how."

"That's a big step, James."

Felicity crossed her legs and looked to the sky. A moment later she continued, "I think you should write them a letter and tell them everything that's on your mind. They may never read it or respond, but you'll know you sent it and it will help make you feel better."

James's lips curled up into a brief smile. "I'm not sure what to write. Can you help me?"

"Absolutely. Let's get some paper."

CHAPTER THIRTY-FOUR

F elicity and James moved into the kitchen. She laid out a notebook and pens on the kitchen table. For the next hour, he poured his soul into the letter—the anguish of believing he would lose his brother and the way that pain instantly flared into a desire for revenge. James included that now he understands what he did was wrong. He was sorry for losing his temper and shooting their son.

Felicity read the note and suggested a couple of edits. When James returned it to her the second time, she told him it was perfect.

"I'll get this to Mrs. Sawyer so she can review it and mail it to the victim's family."

Felicity shuttled between her sister's house, the hospital, and FireSky ranch while Rick stayed at Saint David Medical Center. He only came home to shower, change clothes, and have briefings with Sergio about ranch operations. Felicity checked the mail every day at the ranch to see if the letter James wrote to the victim's family received a response.

Ten days after James wrote his letter, Felicity found an envelope in the mailbox addressed to James Edmunds with a return address in Louisiana. Felicity gasped. The letter felt far heavier than the thin envelope she carried into the farmhouse.

After Felicity and James finished dinner, she pushed across the table the off-white envelope with James's name handwritten in blue ink across the front. James opened the letter and glanced up at Felicity when he saw the contents.

"Go ahead and read it. I'm here if you need me."

Felicity watched James as he carefully read each word. The paper shook as his hands moved further down the page.

When James reached the bottom of the letter, he shook his head. "No, no!" He threw down the letter, put his elbows on the table, and buried his face in his hands.

James continued to yell "No!" into his hands. Felicity grabbed her cell phone off the counter and opened the Sure Cuffs app.

Yelling turned to sobbing.

He rocked back and forth, continuing to weep and choke "No!"

"What's wrong? I can't help you if you don't talk to me."

James looked up and threw the letter across the table to Felicity.

"Read it."

Felicity read the letter from the victim's parents. She wiped away each tear as it passed her cheek and settled on her chin.

We've been hoping we'd get a letter like this from you. Not a day goes by that we don't think of Darryl. We miss his smile, his laugh, and his hugs. We also think of you. We wonder if you are sorry for what you did. We wonder if your family misses you too.

We take no satisfaction that you are in prison. Our son is gone forever and your brother is in a wheelchair. We'd do anything to redo the day that changed all of our lives forever so you both could walk among us today. So that your brother could still walk, too.

. . .

Darryl is in heaven now, and we will see him again. We're sure of it, and that gives us hope. We also have hope you'll find Jesus if you haven't already. He died for our sins when we didn't deserve it. Eternal life is available to us through Jesus if we want it.

It is our decision to extend the same grace to you. We forgive you, Mr. Edmunds. We only hope that you'll do the same and forgive others, including Darryl and yourself.

We accept your apology!

God bless,
Leon and April Griffin

Felicity dabbed her eyes with a tissue. The beauty of it over-whelmed her, yet it was also like a jab in the sore spot of her conflict with Rick.

She walked over to James, who sat in his chair with a dazed look. "This is good news, James; they forgave you."

James looked up. His eyes were full of red streaks. "I don't understand how they could forgive me. I killed their son."

Felicity put her hand on James's shoulder. "I know. It's hard to understand. They did it for you because they know you are in pain, and that their son was not blameless in what happened that night, but they also did it for themselves."

"What do you mean?"

"Resentment and bitterness toward someone will eat you alive. The only way to get rid of it is to forgive the person that hurt you, even if they don't deserve it. They understand we all received grace from God through Jesus, who took the punishment we deserve. His death cancelled the debt for all our sins. Jesus died to wash away our sins even though we didn't deserve it. That's grace and they want to extend grace to you. It doesn't mean what you did was okay, but they are saying you no longer owe them anything. The weight of debt is off your shoulders and theirs."

"Can I go to my room now?"

"Sure."

Before James retired to his room, Felicity received permission to take the letter to the hospital to show Rick. She knew he could use the encouragement during this dark time.

It stung to consider how much she also needed to offer forgiveness.

It was a warm fall day, so Rick and Felicity went for a walk outside the hospital. They found a bench underneath some large live oak trees, and Felicity handed Rick the letter.

"James received this from the victim's family. He was upset after reading it."

Rick held the letter with both hands and read it. As his eyes moved his eyes further down the short letter, his jaw dropped. "Wow."

"I know. It hit James hard."

"I can see why. They took forgiveness to a whole new level I didn't think was possible."

Rick held the letter and looked deep into the second paragraph. He didn't see the words by Leon and April Griffin. He saw his brother Jack. Rick's bitterness felt trivial compared to what Darryl's parents experienced, and they could still forgive their son's killer.

"It puts things in perspective. Kinda makes you think."

"About what?" Felicity inquired.

"About ourselves. About how petty some of our issues seem

when we look at the big picture."

Felicity nodded in agreement.

"It made me think of Jack. I've been so mad at him for so long that sometimes I forget why I don't like him. It's just the way it is now."

"It doesn't have to be that way."

"I know." Rick read the letter one last time.

Felicity put the letter back into her purse. "I should head back to the ranch now to check on James."

Rick walked Felicity to her car and gave her a quick hug. He was thankful she let him touch her again. Maybe all this talk of forgiveness was helping her, too. He waved as she left and went back to the ICU waiting room, whispering a prayer for God to help heal their marriage.

Twelve days passed since Elizabeth had her stroke and everyone had returned to their lives except Rick, Cassie, and Jack. Cassie slept at home at night and came to the hospital for several hours each day. Jack, like Rick, had been at the hospital the entire time except for short breaks to eat, change clothes and shower at the ranch.

The instinct to compete with Jack was immense, even with his mother lying in a coma twenty yards down the hall and the ranch on the brink of being lost. He couldn't sleep at home until Jack did.

Rick considered whether he should apologize to Jack. The thought alone had his stomach doing somersaults. It was not a familiar feeling for Rick, but he recognized it. It was guilt.

Dr. Pavlock interrupted Rick's thoughts and invited all of Elizabeth's children to her office after her next stop. They all waited outside her door until she arrived.

"Please sit down," Dr. Pavlock said as she took a seat behind her desk.

Dr. Pavlock placed her hands on her desk and faced the threesome.

"I'm sorry, but we've done all we can do for your mom here.

Her stroke was severe, and her brain went without oxygen for too long. Her heart and lungs continue to work on their own, but she may never regain consciousness again. We need to transfer her to a facility that can take better care of her in her condition."

Cassie threw herself into Jack's open arms and sobbed. Rick wiped away the steady stream escaping his tear ducts. Cassie turned and hugged Rick. They cried together.

Once they processed the shock of the recommendation, they turned back to Dr. Pavlock, the brothers flanking Cassie, arm in arm.

"Okay, we're ready," Cassie said, drying her tears.

They discussed the detailed steps of a transfer and what to expect from Elizabeth at her new facility. It was only seven blocks down the road from Saint David Medical Center, so it was close to Cassie and Rick. Dr. Pavlock offered her email if anyone had questions and excused herself to attend to another patient.

Jack, Cassie, and Rick returned to the waiting room. Cassie cried yet again and Jack put his arm around her. Nobody spoke, processing the stunning news that their mother might never wake up. She might never see her children or grandchildren again.

Regret for unsaid thoughts and feelings pierced Rick's gut like an arrow. His mental list of things he would say if he ever got the chance grew. It could be too late.

Rick looked over at Jack. His brother's eyes were bloodshot. Rick has never seen much emotion from Jack. It moved him. For a split second, he thought about hugging Jack, but couldn't move from his chair.

Jack was the first to speak when he stood up. "Guys, I'm heading out tomorrow. I need to take care of some things at home, so I'm catching a flight in the morning. We know what will happen to mom now and both of you can handle it from here. I'll come back if something changes."

Cassie thanked Jack for all his sacrifices and support. Rick managed one curt nod of agreement.

Rick drove to FireSky for dinner and a change of clothes.

Felicity returned to her sister's house, so before dinner, Rick toured the equipment barn. Everything looked ready for sale, except the John Deere utility tractor.

"What the heck?" he muttered to the tractor.

Rick called Sergio. "What's up with the utility tractor? I have to sell that in a few days."

"Alex was off for the last week. His wife had their baby early, but his in-laws have come to help her, so he's coming back tomorrow, and we'll pitch in to get it ready for sale."

"Count me in too, Sergio. It's all hands-on-deck for that tractor. It's the reason for this sale."

After dinner, James went to his room to read, and Rick slipped outside. He started a fire in the fire pit and sat by himself. He only moved to add a new log. He thought about his mom and how strong she'd been during the difficult times in her life. She was solid and steady as a granite statue yet as comforting as a warm blanket on a cold winter night. Rick's mind drifted to the letter and Little Jack. Scenes of missed opportunities to forgive and heal flashed through his mind.

Rick left and went into the supply shed. He rummaged around until he found what he was looking for. Rick returned to the fire pit and plopped down in his chair. He put on his thirty-two-year-old baseball glove and slammed his right fist into the webbing liked he'd done a thousand times before.

A few seconds later he removed the glove. He turned it over and pulled at some of the old leather straps. Rick stared at the worn leather inside the mitt and stood up. He raised his right arm slowly, as if he were lifting a heavy weight and released his grip. The glove made a light thud when it hit the burning logs.

Rick stood motionless next to the fire. He watched every fiber ignite and wilt inside the gold flames. Once the glove was reduced to ashes, Rick wobbled back to his chair and sat down.

He leaned back until he could see the stars. "I forgive you."

CHAPTER THIRTY-FIVE

After midnight, Rick returned to the hospital and snuck back into Elizabeth's room. He curled up on the small couch he'd made his bed for the past two weeks. He couldn't sleep, but this time it wasn't because of the new noises in the hospital or the uncomfortable sleeping conditions. It was Jack. Rick kept thinking about the letter to the Griffins and the strength it must have taken James to apologize.

The next morning, Jack packed up and prepared to leave for the airport. He walked over to Rick before leaving the waiting room. "Take good care of mom and let me know if anything changes."

"I will."

Jack waved goodbye and headed out of the waiting room.

"Hey, Jack, how are you getting to the airport?" Rick called after him.

"I'll take a cab from the lobby."

"Give me a minute to get packed up. I'll take you."

The Powell brothers were alone in a vehicle together for the first time since Jack moved to Kansas City. For fifteen minutes, the only sound inside the car came from the cars whizzing past them on the freeway. When Rick saw the signs for the airport exit, he swallowed hard and adjusted his weight. He asked how Jack's wife and kids were doing and heard the same story Jack had shared a dozen times over the past two weeks.

The airport was still sleeping, so Rick pulled in front of the terminal. Jack hopped out as soon as the truck came to a complete stop. He leaned into the open passenger door window.

"Thanks for the ride."

Jack walked toward the terminal doors.

Rick leaped out of the truck, calling, "Jack, wait!"

Jack stopped and turned around as Rick jogged up to him.

"I know you've got to catch your flight, but I have to tell you something first."

They both moved to the side, and Jack put his bags down.

"I'm sorry I've been distant and cold over the years. You were dad's favorite and I've always been jealous. When grandpa died and you left the ranch when we needed you most, it pushed me over the edge. It's eaten me up inside ever since. I don't want to live like this anymore, so I forgive you and I hope you can do the same for me."

Jack put his hand on Rick's shoulder.

"I'm happy to hear your apology, but did you ever consider that I may have left for a good reason?"

Rick shook his head, puzzled. His mouth opened.

"It was like my heart was ripped out of me when dad was killed and then stomped on when grandpa died. I couldn't be there anymore. No way I could spend another second near the ranch, so I got away as fast as I could. When my father-in-law invited me to join his practice in Kansas City, it seemed like the perfect escape. I didn't expect it would be for this long. Time kind of slipped away. I never felt good about leaving, but it's what I had to do at the time."

Rick didn't respond.

"Rick, you should also forgive yourself. I've watched you carrying around that glove and the guilt that dad was driving to see your baseball game the day he died. It wasn't your fault."

"I never blamed myself."

"Then why carry around that glove all these years?"

"It was my prison, but I'm out now. The glove is gone."

Jack tilted his head and furrowed his brow. "Okay, I'm not sure what that means, but I've got to go. Thanks for the apology."

Rick watched Jack grab his bag and disappear into the terminal.

"Thanks for the apology? I hadn't considered that response," Rick muttered as he put the truck into drive. As he drove back to FireSky Ranch, his emotions fluttered up and down. During all the hours Rick had lain awake at night, he envisioned Jack being elated when his younger brother apologized. Past wounds would be buried, and they'd become close. Jack would be the older brother of Rick's dreams.

Despite the unexpected response, Rick was glad he found the courage to apologize and forgive Jack. It felt good for those words to leave his lips and he wondered why he took so long to say them.

The roller coaster ride of emotions ended at the bottom as Rick pulled into FireSky Ranch. It was November first, and he only had two days to fix up and sell enough equipment to stop the auction. He was determined to beat the clock and pay off his past-due balance at Lone Star Bank by November third.

Rick took pictures of all the equipment and placed more ads on local websites and social media groups that ranchers visited to find used equipment. He planned to start the sale at 9:00 a.m. and sell everything in the morning. That would give him enough time to get down to Lone Star Bank and deliver the check personally to Mr. Bartolo. Everything was working as planned.

Early the morning of the planned sale, the FireSky crew moved the equipment from the barn to the parking lot for easier viewing for the buyers. Everything was in place, but when Sergio tried to drive the John Deere utility tractor to the viewing area, the star of the show wouldn't start. Sergio called Alex to help get it started. James also came to help.

Alex tried to get the tractor started several times, but he also failed. The buyers would arrive in less than an hour, so Alex got creative. He told everyone to stand back, and he sprayed ether into the air intake and turned the ignition. It worked. The engine sputtered, and a cloud of exhaust smoke filled the barn.

James moved closer to the tractor to celebrate the good news when a radiator coil burst. A plume of super-heated steam and smoke engulfed James and he rolled on the ground in pain.

Alex jumped off the tractor to help James. As he neared, James rose to his feet, pushed Alex and ran away. James stopped at the opposite end of the barn. He leaned against a fence and slumped over. His eyes were glossy, and his breathing was heavy.

Alex followed James, calling after him, "James, buddy, are you okay?"

But when Alex caught up with him, James grabbed Alex by his shirt collar. He dragged the smaller man several steps over to the wall and pushed him into it. When Alex would attempt to move away from the wall, James would push him back against it. Every time Alex tried to escape, James yelled, "Halt, I said halt!"

Hearing the commotion, the rest of the crew rushed to the scene and saw James pushing Alex. Together they pulled James away so Alex could escape.

James quickly broke free from their grip and dashed out of the barn into the parking area. He looked wildly around the parking lot and, seeing a worker's truck, jumped in. James sped off into the south end of the ranch. The rest of the crew followed in their trucks.

James pulled to a stop in the south end of FireSky Ranch and emerged with a rifle from the gun rack in the cab's back window.

Alex was the first member of the FireSky crew to exit his truck. He saw James marching up the bluff and pursued him.

Once Alex was thirty feet away, he yelled, "Come on back, James. It's okay."

James turned and looked over his shoulder. Alex could see his wide eyes and muscles straining in his neck. Alex continued to jog toward James until he roared, "Don't come near me!"

The long rifle in James's right hand caught Alex by surprise. He stopped, gasped, "Oh no!" then retreated. As he approached the team standing near their trucks, he shouted, "He has a gun!"

They all scurried behind their trucks until Alex arrived.

"What should we do?"

Alex held up his hand until he caught his breath. "Something is wrong with James and he's armed. We need to call 911."

CHAPTER THIRTY-SIX

R ick looked out the kitchen window and wondered why nobody was moving equipment into the parking lot. He pulled out his phone and before he could dial, a call from Sergio appeared. He explained the situation with James. Rick looked to the clock. It was a quarter past eight.

"Come on. Not now, James."

Rusty Red transported Rick to the south end. Sergio and his crew met Rick as he parked, and they explained what happened with James. He saw him sitting on the top of the bluff with a rifle.

Three minutes later, members of the sheriff's department showed up in two SUVs. Sergio and Alex had returned to the sale, but the other FireSky workers pointed to James on the bluff, two hundred yards away. The deputies quickly took defensive positions behind their vehicles.

Rick met with one deputy hunkered down near the back bumper and explained he was the owner of the ranch and that James was an inmate placed through the TDCJ RIHARP program.

"So we have a convicted felon from Huntsville on a hill with a loaded rifle about two hundred yards away from here. Did I get that right?

"It's more complicated than that."

"What's he in for?"

"Uh, you don't want to know."

The deputy slipped into his vehicle and called for additional backup. He clicked the button to the mic to speak to the person at the other end of the radio a few times. The deputy gave James a long stare as he sat on the ground with the rifle laying across his legs.

"The sheriff and a TDCJ officer are on his way."

"Who is it?"

"I'm not sure, but dispatch said they'd be here in ten minutes and one vehicle contains a TDCJ officer."

If it was Officer Hartley, Rick knew things could go sideways fast once he arrived. He came up with a plan.

Rick told the deputies about Sure Cuffs and his plan to activate them. He tried the mobile app first, but it didn't work. He didn't have a signal strong enough in that isolated part of the ranch. Rick moved to plan B. The deputy turned on the loudspeaker in his SUV and handed Rick the mic.

"Wookie."

"Wookie."

"Wookie!"

Rick tried the emergency word several more times, but James continued to sit on the top of the hill, unaffected by Sure Cuffs.

"It must be the wind, or he's too far away," Rick muttered.

The deputies turned to watch two more SUVs from the sheriff's office arrive at FireSky Ranch with their lights flashing but sirens silent.

Rick recognized the first man to get out of the first vehicle: the county sheriff. And then, as he feared, Officer Bryan Hartley got out of the rear passenger seat.

Officer Hartley walked with the sheriff over to the deputies crouched behind the Ford Explorer with the sheriff's emblem on the door. Rick couldn't hear what they were talking about, but he guessed it was not favorable for him or James. Rick moseyed over to the four men to hear their conversation.

As expected, Officer Hartley attempted to whip the deputies into a frenzy. "He's not stable, and he's dangerous. He's killed before, and he has PTSD. I don't know how much longer he'll remain calm, so I'd advise your team to take positions for a shot if he gets aggressive."

The others nodded and reached for their firearms, so Rick knew his time to help James was limited.

Another vehicle pulled up to the scene. It was Felicity's white Ford Explorer. As soon as she got out, the deputies yelled at her to get down. She gave them the withering look she usually used when her children said something outrageous. Then she scurried over to Rick.

"What's going on? What are they going to do?"

"I was making progress with the deputies before Hartley arrived and got them all riled up. He's making James out to be some crazed lunatic just waiting to explode."

"Did you try activating Sure Cuffs?"

"Yeah, my signal is not strong enough for the app to work and he's also out of range for the emergency word. We even tried the loudspeaker."

"You need to get closer."

"What?" He couldn't have heard her right. Closer was ultimate foolishness. He was unarmed.

Felicity and Rick turned around when they saw two deputies move from behind their vehicles and dart into the tree line at the bottom of the bluff. They separated and moved about fifty feet from each other. Both laid prone with their rifles aimed at James. Sniper position.

"You need to get closer to James, so you can activate Sure Cuffs with the emergency word."

"I don't know." Rick felt the blood drain from his face and he ran his hand through his hair several times as his gaze moved from loaded gun to loaded gun. One wrong move and it would all be over for him, for FireSky Ranch.

Officer Hartley's voice came out of the loudspeaker. "James

Edmunds, put the gun down and proceed toward the vehicles with your hands high in the air."

James didn't move.

"Rick, they will shoot him. You need to get closer to James so you can use the emergency word. James is angry with himself, not any of us."

The speaker crackled again. "James Edmunds, you need to comply with these commands. Put the gun down and your hands up."

Rick looked at Felicity. Tears welled in her eyes. Her look of dread was all the convincing he needed. Rick marched up the hill toward James.

CHAPTER THIRTY-SEVEN

Rick heard officers shouting at him, "Get back. You can't go up there. Get back here now!"

However, he had no intention of turning around. He needed to reach James.

James watched Rick march up the bluff and didn't move until he was fifty feet away. James got to his feet and yelled, "Don't come any closer!"

Rick continued toward James. He hoped that James understood he was coming to help him. Rick said a quick prayer. *Father, please give me the wisdom to do and say the right thing for James. Let us both emerge from this situation unharmed.*

When Rick got within twenty feet, James swung the rifle from the horizontal position to a vertical position. He pointed the barrel under his chin.

"Don't make me do this," James called, his voice hitching. "I'll end this right now."

Rick didn't even slow down. Although his legs felt heavier and weaker with each step, he continued. He had to reach James, physically and emotionally.

James put his index finger inside the trigger guard. With his long arms, it wasn't the least bit awkward. And after two tours in Iraq, he knew his way around a gun.

Rick's heart hammered. He thrust his hand up with his palm facing James. "Don't do it!"

"I don't deserve to live. I'll be doing everybody a favor if I pull this trigger," James roared with spittle spraying from his lips.

Beads of sweat fell from James's flaring nostrils, so Rick slowed his advance.

When Rick could almost touch James, he murmured, "Darryl's family gave you a gift. They forgave you even when they didn't have to. That's the definition of true grace, and it's your turn to share it."

James's shoulders relaxed but kept the gun barrel pointed under his chin.

Rick said, "We don't have a lot of time, James. The deputies are nervous with you holding a loaded rifle. They could shoot at any time."

James looked around, surveying the deputies in the tree line with their rifle barrels pointed toward him.

Rick continued to press James, "I need to forgive a few people too. Let's do this together."

James stared at Rick, his expression full of fear and confusion.

Behind them, Officer Hartley yelled out, "what the heck is Powell doing? We need to disarm the inmate now."

Sweat prickled across Rick's back. He took one more step toward James, so that he was close enough to touch James and look deep into his eyes. Rick saw the confusion and fear.

Officer Hartley turned to the deputies without bothering to turn off the mic. "This is taking too long. I'm heading up there. If the convict gets violent, disarm him by any means necessary." He slammed his microphone down and followed Rick's path up to James.

Rick saw Hartley stalking toward them. He was nearly out of time. Rather than panic, he asked James, "Remember why we call this FireSky Ranch?"

James nodded and lowered the rifle until its barrel pointed to the ground.

"Remember, the past is in the past. Let's get up early and watch a new day start tomorrow. Together."

James looked over at the east hills. He locked his eyes on the eastern sky for half a minute as if he were watching a sunrise.

"Give me the gun," Rick coaxed, "and you can start new right now."

James turned back to Rick and saw Officer Hartley right behind him. James pulled the rifle back toward his face.

In a panic, Rick grabbed the barrel of the rifle and yelled, "Give me the gun!"

Officer Hartley snatched the rifle from Rick's hands and pushed Rick aside with his body.

Startled by Hartley, Rick let go of the barrel. He then grabbed the officer's uniform and tried to wrench him away from James and the gun. Hartley wouldn't let go. Soon all three of them had both hands on the rifle. They danced on the top of the bluff as each pulled hard to win sole access to the weapon. Rick felt the pulls and chose to push Hartley to knock him off James.

A thunderous sound sent all three men to the ground. It was a gunshot from the wood line.

Rick took the opportunity to grab the rifle and scrambled to his feet first. He saw Officer Hartley on his hands and knees. He was looking down and shaking his head as if trying to clear the blast from his ears. James laid motionless, face down in the dirt a few yards from Rick.

Rick tossed the rifle away from them all, waved his arms in the air, and screamed, "Don't shoot!"

He rushed to James's side and turned him over. Rick gasped.

CHAPTER THIRTY-EIGHT

James lay immobilized, his arms tight to his sides, and legs snapped firmly together. He was alive and unhurt, if somewhat in shock. The bullet missed him, but the sound of the deputies' rifles had activated Sure Cuffs.

Rick let out a huge breath. "Praise God."

James blinked at him, bewildered.

"Just stay put for a minute, buddy, while I get these guys to stand down. They'll be less nervous with you held still with the Sure Cuffs."

"Okay," James whispered.

Rick left James on the ground and waved for the sheriff's team to proceed up the hill.

Rick met them with the rifle and handed it over before they reached James. Hartley was several steps behind.

"That was an idiotic thing to do, Mr. Powell," the deputy said.

"Probably," Rick admitted. "But James deserved a chance to hear from someone he trusts. He's secure now in Sure Cuffs, and unhurt."

Felicity grappled him in a bear hug. They held each other tight for a long moment, then walked back to the police vehicles with arms around each other.

"That may have been obstruction, Mr. Powell," Officer Hartley said. "I'll have to look into that when I get back to the office."

Rick shook his head and sighed, "You just don't get it do you? I was about to disarm him without incident until you showed up and interfered. That's gross negligence from a law enforcement officer. You may want to look at that first."

Officer Hartley glared at Rick but did not respond.

Rick and Felicity held hands as they stood by the sheriff's car. They watched the deputies place James into traditional cuffs and lowered his head into the back of the police vehicle.

Rusty Red pulled into the site of the equipment sale just before noon. Sergio explained that the shoppers all left when multiple sheriff's vehicles whizzed through the ranch with lights and sirens. They'd sold two saddles and a tiller, but nothing more.

Tomorrow was the deadline, and Rick had no way to pay off his outstanding balance to stop the auction.

On November fourth, Rick took his time getting out of bed. He was careful not to disturb Felicity. It was Saturday and the weekend crew hadn't yet arrived. He poured himself a second cup of coffee and savored each warm sip.

He left the farmhouse and took Rusty Red for a short ride. One-hundred thirty-four steps past the cemetery gate, he arrived at his father's granite marker. Rick stared for several minutes at the letters that formed Jack Powell Sr. etched into the stone. He paced back and forth.

Rick spun and turned to face his father. "I'm sorry, Dad. I know I never should have held a grudge against Little Jack. It's gone on for too long."

He stopped pacing for an instant when he saw another car pull into the small gravel parking lot. Once Rick saw they weren't headed his direction, he paced in front of his father's marker again.

"I'm sorry for losing the ranch. At the time I thought I was doing the right things to keep the place afloat, but nothing worked. I didn't want to let anyone else know I was struggling, especially Little Jack."

Rick watched the visitor kneel in front of a tombstone near the cemetery entrance.

"The good news is that I forgave Jack and told him I was sorry. I don't know if it helped, but I'm glad I did it. It has lifted a huge weight off my shoulders."

Rick walked up to the monument and placed his right hand on top.

"I'll come visit you after we find a new place. Bye, Dad."

Rick slapped the top of the granite like he always did, but this time with his bare hand. He stood silent and closed his eyes. Ten minutes later he left the cemetery.

Rick returned to the farmhouse and started packing. Soon he'd be homeless.

Monday morning, November sixth, Felicity received a call from Mrs. Sawyer. She asked if she could visit FireSky Ranch to get more details on the incident with James. They agreed to a 1:00 p.m. meeting. Felicity met Mrs. Sawyer at the end of the sidewalk and led her up to the porch. Rick joined them, and the three of them made themselves comfortable.

Felicity spoke first. "So how can we help you today?"

"Well, the RIHARP Discipline Review Board has scheduled a hearing on Wednesday to review disciplinary action against James Edmunds and his eligibility to be part of the RIHARP program. During the hearing, they'll hear testimony from the RIHARP program manager and any other TDCJ stakeholders before they make their decision."

"Can Rick and I come and testify on his behalf?"

"No, not at these board meetings. It's just for TDCJ employees, support staff, and contractors, so that's why I'm going."

"So much for a right to due process in front of a jury of your peers," Rick grumbled.

"Mr. Powell, this isn't a trial. Mr. Edmunds committed a crime as an inmate serving a sentence, so he's subject to the TDCJ review board. They are his judge and jury."

"How can we help?" Felicity inquired.

"James is facing additional time to his sentence, and I'm hoping to keep that to a minimum. I also want to keep him in the RIHARP program because I think this is the best place for him. It's a long shot, but I will try."

Mrs. Sawyer, Felicity, and Rick discussed the incident—and James's growth during his time on FireSky Ranch—until evening shadows engulfed the porch.

Rick didn't have the heart to tell Mrs. Sawyer they would soon no longer have a ranch to host James.

CHAPTER THIRTY-NINE

On Friday, November tenth, Rick got up early. He loaded some additional boxes into Rusty Red, then walked the ranch grounds one last time. At 9:30 a.m., Rick saw one truck approaching the ranch on the gravel road and another some distance behind.

"Must be the auctioneers."

A silver Nissan Titan pickup truck pulled into the parking lot like the driver owned the place. After the dust settled, Rick recognized the person getting out of the truck, and his jaw dropped.

It was his brother Jack. Rick hadn't seen or talked to him since his apology a week ago. Rick slinked over to Jack as he climbed down from the truck. "I wished we could have worked things out sooner. The auction for FireSky is taking place today. I imagine that truck not too far behind you is the auctioneer."

"Are you serious? I came all the way out here for a good auction, and now I don't get to see it happen?"

Rick tilted his head and furrowed his brow. "What do you mean you don't get to see it happen?"

"There isn't going to be an auction for FireSky. That debt is paid in full."

"I don't understand. How is that possible?"

"Well, you know how I've always been the favorite son?"

Rick punched Jack in the arm. "Shut up, don't remind me."

"I've had access to the FireSky account since Grandpa died but haven't looked at it in years. After our talk, I spoke with Cass, and she told me about the lake house. I figured you were in serious financial trouble, so I checked the account."

Rick rubbed the back of his neck and with a sheepish grin responded, "Impressive wasn't it? Bet you never saw anyone lose money so fast."

"I called Lone Star Bank, and they connected me with some guy, and he said FireSky was going up for auction."

"Was it Bartolo?"

"Yeah, he told me that if we didn't pay the outstanding balance by the third, the auction would take place today. It was the second, so I wired the money to cover the overdue balance and added a little extra to give you some breathing room."

Rick's lips quivered. "I can't believe you'd do that for me."

"I know I'm not innocent in all this. It was wrong of me to abandon you all those years ago. But I didn't take care of the debt just for you, little brother, I did it for us. This is our family ranch, and I want it to remain that way. Powells investing in Powells."

"Thanks, Jack, this means a lot."

"I hope you can continue to run this place now that you get another chance. You had a plan and gave it your all. I admire that. I know you've learned a lot from your mistakes and believe with a little more support from Cassie and me, you can make FireSky as great as you want it to be."

Rick felt like he could float. He'd just gained the approval he'd been seeking for as long as he could remember. The next vehicle pulled into the parking lot as Rick hugged Jack. The black GMC Yukon rolled to a stop and idled.

"I see you've got company, so I'll go pay Cassie a visit. I'll be back this afternoon."

Rick waved to Jack Jr. and turned his attention to the new vehicle on his property.

A uniformed TDCJ officer got out of the Yukon. He stopped when he saw Rocky barking in front of the SUV.

"How can I help you?" Rick asked, grasping his dog's collar.

"Mr. Powell? I have information to share regarding the RIHARP investigation on James Edmunds."

Rick directed Rocky to the porch, where Felicity now stood, likely drawn by the barking.

Rick motioned to the officer it was safe to move from behind the car. His mind was racing with questions. Why did they send an officer instead of calling with the results of the hearing? Was the news so bad they wanted to send someone to deliver it in person? Did Officer Hartley convince the board he did something wrong? Should he call a lawyer?

"Mr. Powell, the RIHARP Discipline Review Board met earlier this week and listened to several hours of testimony. They deliberated for hours and came to a unanimous decision."

Felicity walked down the steps and stood next to Rick so she could hear the revelation.

"They determined that James Edmunds was guilty of unlawful possession of a firearm by a convicted felon, so they added eighteen months to his sentence."

Felicity put her hands over her face, and Rick gave her a side hug. Poor James. More time lost.

"They also agreed with RIHARP counselor Kimberly Sawyer that James Edmunds is still a good candidate for full rehabilitation and reentry into society under the RIHARP program as long as he is living here and continues to receive mental health treatment."

Felicity's hands dropped from her face.

"If you're willing to host Mr. Edmunds as part of the RIHARP program, I can release him back into your custody."

"Right now?" Felicity asked.

"Yes, ma'am. He's in the vehicle with my partner right now."

Felicity jumped up and down, "Yes, yes, we'll take him back!"

The officer walked back to the Yukon and opened the door. James sat for a moment, staring, then slid out of the SUV. Felicity hugged James first, and then Rick followed. Rocky left the porch and came down to welcome James back to FireSky Ranch.

CHAPTER FORTY

Two weeks later, Rick and Felicity prepared to host their kids for Thanksgiving dinner later that week. Rick finally shared the financial details of the business, all of them, with Felicity. She surprisingly offered to help him manage the day-to-day bookkeeping, something she used to do for Dr. Shelton when she was his office manager. The extra money from Jack Jr. combined with the RIHARP payments would help FireSky avoid falling back into debt.

Rick called a meeting with the FireSky crew. Felicity and James joined Sergio and his team near the training pen.

"I have good news. We are in better financial shape now and are close to a point where we can finally let Sergio retire so Anna can get him back. If we can lease six more stalls, we can hire a general manager for FireSky Ranch."

"Is that when you'll start your new agency?" Felicity asked.

"I've called off the plan to start a new agency. I have some freelance consulting lined up, but this is my new career. Rancher and co-owner of FireSky Ranch."

Felicity grabbed Rick's hand and smiled.

Rick looked to the crew. "I'm going to launch a new ad

campaign next week, and I'd appreciate it if you could also help get the word out. With your help, I know we can find six more boarders."

"You bet, boss!" Alex called out. The rest of the crew nodded in agreement.

"Thanks, team. We're in this together."

As the crew dispersed to return to their tasks, an unfamiliar truck pulled into FireSky Ranch.

Two men got out. They both wore shirts with the sleeves torn off, ripped jeans, and work boots. The younger one was covered with neck tattoos, and the older man had a long graying beard braided like a Viking warrior.

Rick met them as they walked toward the stables. "Can I help you?"

"I heard you have a convict living and working here."

Rick's brow narrowed and the muscles in his neck and shoulders tightened. Where these guys here to cause trouble?

Rick looked around. "Nope, no convict here."

"Then who's that?" The men said, pointing at James.

Felicity took a step in front of James.

Rick scanned both men carefully before he replied. "That's James Edmunds; he's my assistant general manager for FireSky Ranch. He's on loan from the Texas Department of Criminal Justice for a few more years, but after that, he may become the full-time general manager."

Rick looked back and saw a wide smile from James, revealing his missing tooth. Rick smiled in return. He loved that gap-toothed smile.

"Thank you, Mr. Powell," James called.

"Please call me Rick."

The bearded man said, "I heard he's good with horses."

"One of the best."

Neck tattoo guy took a step forward. He extended his hand to Rick and they shook hands. "I'm Aaron. I'm with a Christian nonprofit organization called Freedom Pathways. We help reintroduce former inmates back into society through a program that teaches accountability, faith, responsibility, and general life skills. Too many former inmates recommit crimes because they're not prepared for life on the outside. We help teach them to follow the right paths for long-term freedom."

Rick nodded in agreement. "Sounds like a great organization."

"Your set up here with the horses, chickens, and garden couldn't be any better for us. They are perfect for our program."

Rick looked over at Felicity and tipped his hat. She returned a deep smile and a salute.

"Our goal is to help them make the most of their second chance because they may not get another one."

"It's their last second chance," the bearded man added.

"How can we help you?" Rick asked as Felicity and James came and stood by his side.

"We need a place to board our horses that will also allow these men and women to work with the staff on the grounds, learning new skills until they graduate. They will do any dirty work you need around here. You name it. We pay the boarding fees and former inmates' wages through our generous donors. They stay at a group home ten minutes up the road."

Rick's lips curved upward.

"So far we haven't had any luck finding a partner. We're hoping you would understand the benefits we provide better than the others and consider a year lease for our horses and tasks for these former inmates to take on."

Rick turned to Felicity and James. Felicity smiled, and James nodded with his approval.

"We can do that. How many stalls do you need?"

"Nine."

"Nine?" Rick asked for confirmation.

"Yes, sir."

Rick turned to face Felicity as her smile grew wide. She

wrapped her arms around his waist and leaned her head on his chest.

"We'd be honored to host your program here," Rick told Aaron.

James nodded. "Every day is a fresh start at FireSky Ranch."

THE END

RATE THIS BOOK

I f you enjoyed *Last Second Chance*, please consider providing a review on Amazon or Goodreads for it. It doesn't have to be elaborate or even very long. Simply share what you thought of the book. Reviews help readers decide if they would like to purchase a book or not and is useful feedback for me.

MORE BOOKS BY ROBERT GOLUBA

HOPE REFRESHED

A college football fan is beaten and left for dead on the side of a parking lot. A bank president is getting rich gouging consumers. A software developer finds a homeless shelter for his next hot meal.

Will they turn around their dire situations? Or fall deeper into despair?

Hope Refreshed brings six Bible parables back to life again as they are retold as modern, inspirational stories.

Learn more about *Hope Refreshed* on Amazon.

ABOUT THE AUTHOR

Robert Goluba is an author of Christian suspense and inspirational fiction. He published *Hope Refreshed* in 2016 and Last Second Chance, a Christian suspense novel in June 2019. Robert was born and raised in Central Illinois, where he attended college, served in the Army National Guard, and met his wife. At age thirty, after a self-diagnosed allergy to snow, he moved to sunny Arizona

He continues to live in the Phoenix area with his wonderful wife, two kids, and canine companion.

Email Newsletter

For new release updates, exclusive promotions and freebies, sign up for Robert Goluba's author email newsletter at: RobertGoluba.com/newsletter

Made in the USA
Middletown, DE
24 June 2020

10805224R00146